T0063915

Nothing Is Real

Samuel Hathy

authorHOUSE®

AuthorHouse™
1663 Liberty Drive
Bloomington, IN 47403
www.authorhouse.com
Phone: 1-800-839-8640

Published by AuthorHouse 11/11/2014

ISBN: 978-1-4969-5191-5 (sc)
ISBN: 978-1-4969-5190-8 (e)

Hisako's Journal

In a moment there was a ringing in my ears and enlightenment in my head. The songs from the Heavens or whatever they are called were absorbed by an impressionable mind and then all the answers in the universe were mine. Endless desire couldn't nourish my hunger, nor knowledge or power. The best thing to do would have been ironically sacrifice it all and do nothing at all, but observe what will be because everything is preordained; to sit like a Buddha with inches of space to live and endless contemplations, dimensions, and places to witness without even the move of a square inch or whichever measurement you would prefer whilst reading this entry if anyone is alive to even see it. It was all in my grasp but the more one travels, the more one tries, the more one learns the more everything seems confused and lost. Everything is doomed, always was, always will be and no one is to blame. It is neither a God, nor the people living their lives. As I write the whole world has turned against me; its people are coming in waves of hundreds, but as they get closer they vanish in my midst. I am not controlling this it is just the way it had to happen. Whole countries and continents will be swallowed in my presence. Once everything is gone I wonder if I should continue a new world so these catastrophes can happen again. Only time will tell, whatever that is.

I

"Oh Jesus yes, oh, oh my god, you know how to treat a woman!" screamed a woman nearing her middle ages. Her lover was thrusting and making love like lovers do, felt the passion but the man atop her was not thinking of her. His mind wasn't even in the present time. His body was focused on her, but his mind was elsewhere. How insulted she may have been if she knew. It was doubtful however she had no heart to break she seemed only an object that only lived for pleasure. She was a hedonist and an aesthetic. She only lived for herself and pleasures. She was the man's wife but she was not committed like one was expected to be; to be fair her husband wasn't either. Neither of the two really had actual jobs but they were set for life. The husband was capable of predicting the stock market and could become rich off it and didn't bother with anything else. His wife had only five functions.

1. Sitting at home and watch brain numbing sitcoms and "reality television".
2. Shopping
3. Drinking
4. Sex and parties
5. Singing along to her favorite pop, rock, and country songs….. badly.

This was the list her husband made one time they had an argument and they tried an exercise their psychiatrist told them to practice where they were told to write about things the other spouse was good at. Obviously the husband did this in mocking disgust of his wife. There wasn't really much else to work from to be honest.

Just now the wife had noticed that the expression on her husband's face was showing that he wasn't focused on her. She pushed him off of her and he made no reaction to this; even when she pushed with enough force to knock him of the bed they had been making love on if you wish to call it that. He just sat there, staring into the wall as if he was descending into the sea like the maelstrom in Edgar Poe's tale or into some kind of abyss. He wasn't so much staring at anything really however; it was more like he was sleeping with his eyes open. He was in some respect because he was incapable of seeing anything aside from his dream or the visions of the past. Some might say his life was flashing before his very eyes. It could not however that phrase associates to someone who is on their death bed. This man however was immortal and wasn't capable of death. He was not always like this; there was a time when he was very human. Many would even consider him a bum or useless inhabitant of space. Most suspected he would not live past the age of fifty for his lifestyle was dangerous and would ruin anyone (any normal person). As he was making intercourse he pictured a birth but not of a future son he would have but of himself.

"WAAAAAAA!" screamed a little baby but it was not intended to happen. The parents he was born with didn't want him and begged the doctor to perform an abortion. They couldn't abort their child themselves so they were determined to send it away. They did eventually, within the third year of his birth. He was sent to an orphanage where he was quickly adopted surprisingly; within a few more years by a family desperate to have one. It was ironic in a sense that his own family didn't want him, but by strangers he was the holy grail (not literal of course). The parents were desperate, the wife couldn't become fertile and they really wanted a child to show off to all their fellow church goers. Their father particularly was interested in showing off their son. He would now pretend that this adopted child was some miracle of his own sperm when in fact it wasn't. His wife wanted to talk about the labours and joys of motherhood with the other church wives during their book clubs and other functions that the church had. They wanted a name to reflect what they wanted for the child. They were superstitious that way. His name was Hisako, their parents weren't Japanese or even part Japanese but the child they adopted was and wanted to keep the exotic feel to the name as if they had adopted him from some desperate poor country to give the poor soul a better life. This was another part of their sucking up to the church and maintaining an image of spiritual exceptionalism. The name meant "long living" as in prosperous like a king or something like that is what they had thought when they picked the name. Throughout his life they put impossible standards or expectations for their child. They told him things like "You've got to learn how to smile as you kill if you want to be like the folks on the hill." (Lennon, 1971(US) 1975(UK)) They didn't say this but more or less it is what they meant.

"Wake up you sleeping bastard!" screamed Hisako's wife in the present and after moments of this he finally gave into her hopes. Well, if one could say she could have hopes. She was already living them; sleeping around with random guys along with her husband, drinking and pretty much everything as long as it satisfied her lusts or passions though passion would be too respectful a word to be put into relation with this individual. This individual specifically was the wife of Hisako which has been introduced in some detail but her name was different and her last name could be many in a traditional sense; it was Brittany Wilson. Her backstory is mostly uninteresting she was born into mild luxury and had too many addictions which had her descend into poverty. During her childhood the most important goal was to fit in with everyone. She followed fashions and fads and changed with them as they had changed. She almost wasn't a person really; she was more like a walking billboard. She was puppet of the capitalist system, a pawn of product placement, a slave to materialism. To keep a long, uninteresting, sad story short, Brittany was the stereotypical dumb blond that is made jokes about by comedians and everyone that wasn't that themselves. Hisako started yelling at Brittany upon his waking. He said stuff like "Shut up you fucking bitch" and "Why don't you get a job and make something of yourself instead of sleeping around with everyone in town". She pretty much mirrored the mostly unintelligible childlike arguing amongst them. She even called him a bitch. Hisako gave her a few hard smacks in the face and left his home.

"I hate this shit", he muttered outside the large apartment building in which he lived in. Outside were a few strip malls that had half the shops out of business. If you walked a bit down the road you would find a Sam's Club. He made his way towards a bar and "had a tall cold one" as some people would say in attempts to sound folky or nice. "I just don't know what to fucking do anymore!" he said in a slightly louder tone than his previous statement that he in fact "hated this shit". The other people in the bar didn't even turn to look at Hisako; no one knew him really. *I would expect at least one person to be slightly concerned for me*, Hisako thought as he felt sorry for himself much like an emo clique teenager. He even started to cry. He wasn't crying; no tears feel. He felt like doing it though, but he didn't want anyone to see; he was self-conscious that way. "Well what the fuck is your asshole's problem?" he yelled with mild intensity (it wasn't loud but it was filled with a harsh biting release of tension.) Obviously, everyone in the bar was confused to some degree because he was inviting everyone into his problems with pretty much no explanation of them in the first place. "Well what the hell do you want us to do?" a man said in reply in calm soothing tone in an attempt to calm down. It wasn't as soothing or calm as he would have hoped for Hisako only got angrier. "You assholes are just sitting there like nothing is wrong when a man is clearly upset; what if I was fucking suicidal", Hisako yelled. "That isn't really our problem; we don't even fucking know you." one of the men replied. "Forget about this fucking, douche, pussy, bastard, and lets drink somewhere else." a somewhat more obnoxious of the men exclaimed. They were all unsympathetic bastards but Hisako was also a bastard so I guess they belonged together but they parted. The other men just left the bar, and Hisako sat alone with the bartender still remaining (well of course it was his job). "Hey kid, what's the matter?" the bartender asked. "Oh it is nothing." Hisako replied with a sigh of hopelessness uncertainty and also some relief for he already blew off some steam earlier. "Are you sure?" the bartender questioned with some genuine sympathy which was rare for most people to hear "in these days" most old timers would say to make the good old days sound better than the changing times, but in reality I would bet things were mostly the same. These were Hisako's shared thought about genuine sympathy. It really choked him up inside in fact but again he didn't want to give into his emotions again. Most people in his life he felt were "shitting him" as he would say. Everyone was so phony to him: family, friends, religion, and politicians. *It's all so fake* he thought and then he blacked out.

He didn't know what he was seeing. The past? The future? Heaven? Hell? It could be anything but most likely it was a dream. In reality it was long, about an hour. To him it felt very long in the moment and afterwards it really felt like a split second. He was in a dark place with red lighting everywhere and insane crazy people running everywhere, the temperature was nonexistent, and so were any clouds or ceiling. Even when he remembered that he walked into the dark place through a doorway inside a house. There were people trapped in cages they seemed just as crazy as the rest but they wore nice clothes and after thinking about all this he woke up to witness his past again.

He was sitting down with his family drinking a soda. They were watching television, but he wasn't really watching, he was enjoying his soda and disliking his homework. He was the kind of kid whom in school hardly talked to peers and focused on his work. In part from parental guidance, but also that he didn't fit in much with the other kids. He was one of those "goodie two shoed Christian boys" at that time. His parents were watching Glenn Beck, when he was still on Fox News.

Later Hisako made a joke that Glenn Beck was too crazy stupid for Fox that they put him on the Blaze, another extreme right wing propaganda network. This particular family evening was when Hisako was about the age of 15. It was a very uneventful evening like most at the Wilson house. They never really did anything as a family. Hisako's dad said "We never can afford to do anything because Obama and his cronies are taxing the bejesus out of us hardworking American citizens!" well not in such a corny way but almost as much. In any event it was a lame excuse for the Wilson family had plenty of money to do things. The father was a pretty successful corporate banker. It was almost surprising that the father didn't yell at his wife for not having a job because (oh how the wealthy suffer) it is surely a thing to laugh about but anyway, his wife was a stay at home mom. She was sparred the yelling because of the traditional family lifestyle that that family had been. In fact Mr. Wilson got angry at Hisako before his wife, when it came to finding employment and he was only 15 at the time. Mr. Wilson was a flipping sexist; it was obvious. He wasn't the kind that screamed at attractive women at construction sites like a mad dog or the kind that pound on a woman like a drunken idiot but he was the kind of guy that thought it was ok for a man to go around and give people cock every other day but if women showed their cunt to anyone they were a whore, slut, bitch temptress from one of Hell's 9 circles. He also was the kind that thinks women should be pampered and not have to do anything, but housewife things. He was living in the 1950s and even the 50s may have scoffed at his opinions. Also, if the man had a business he would pay woman less most definitely. The wife did work, though in a sense but wasn't paid shit but for some reason she didn't seem to care too much. If she did she certainly was good at keeping it a secret. She cleaned, cooked, did laundry, shopped, did random acts of kindness to certain people. Mrs. Wilson was very devout Christian as opposed to her husband, that only said he was but never read the Bible and only was involved in church to attend Sunday services. He used Christianity to talk bad about the liberal atheists taking religion out of things which was absurd because only paranoid loons believed in these warped stories that everyone was out to get Christians. *How the fuck is it the biggest religion if everyone is out to get Christians more like Christians are out to get everyone else*, thought Hisako as he thought his father viewing his past. But Mrs. Wilson was actually pretty genuine or perhaps more ignorant in her faith or more properly labeled blind faith. *What is real faith anyway? What is anything?* She helped with church functions, read her Bible, and Joyce Meyer books on a regular basis, made food for more needy families, sometimes worked in soup kitchens. She wasn't as stupid ignorant to the poor as Mr. Wilson was. She saw how they had suffered more. Mr. Wilson only read the lips of Glenn Beck and heard the voice of Rush Limbaugh. In addition Mrs. Wilson grew up in a less privileged background. She was still a Republican despite all this somehow. Probably because she shared her husband's view on same sex marriage and pro-choice which were practically the only things that seemed to matter to people during elections in these days. Other than that it was loosely detailed promises about the economy. *It makes me furious when the news and media push the topics of same sex marriage and pro-choice for a politician's platform*, Hisako thought as a child. He was beginning to become annoyed with Glenn Beck. His friends were mostly liberals at school probably because he was amongst the "unpopular" crowd. Liberals seem to have the tendency to be outcasts by society. People that don't think or don't give any damns are the majority of students in schools and they don't know anything about politics. All the conservatives seemed to be dumb rednecks that Hisako didn't want to associate with. He grew up conservatively but he just didn't connect with those imbecilic morons. Hisako left his parents to their show and went to his room to text his friends.

The perspective left from Hisako as he went up the staircase. The Hisako from the future was very much like one of the ghosts in Charles Dickens's A Christmas Carol. He couldn't be seen by anyone in the real world whatever that really was (when there is a man who can leap through timelines through sudden seizures in the present which were self-inflicted). They weren't thoroughly self-made but only when he was annoyed with people or certain conversations he would just blank out. He was just standing there watching his parents watch television. *God, they were so incredibly dull*, he thought. They hardly even spoke to each other. The husband was glued to the television and the wife was stuck in bad literature. He stood there for hours without hardly any disruption it was like a still photo. Sigmund Freud had a theory that a father's son always had fantasies of killing their father and loving the mother. That was incredibly true in part; he did want to kill his father, there was no chance in hell that he would love or marry his mother. They were such great contrasts the two. One was so incredibly dull in one way and the other so much in the other. The father was passionate but wasn't really ambitious. I mean he did a lot but he was married to traditions and conservation (and conservation that wouldn't help the environment). He believed in some kind of American dream but it was only a dream to the wealthy and privileged and a nightmare for the poor and destitute. He wanted women to wear dresses and men to wear ties and top hats. It would be hard for the man to tolerate an African American sharing the same dream or Latin American (basically everything but a WASP; White Anglo Saxon Protestant if it must be spelled out). He didn't want to do anything fantastic; he had no dreams beyond his job as a corporate banker. His wife on the other hand has almost completely no passion or ambition. She was very passive and did whatever her husband told her. His mother probably would become a progressive if not married to such a capitalistic bastard. He beat some sense into her whenever she made any reforms to change with the times. It didn't take much to keep her under control so these altercations happened little. How Hisako looked at his parents with disgust; it made his stomach turn. It made him question how his life would be if he lived with his birth parents. He wondered whether it were for better or worse. *Could it be any other way,* he thought. As soon as the thought crossed his mind he for some reason heard a clock's hands moving in the distance; he could even hear the gears turning. Everything seemed to be moving so slow and every bit of noise seemed so incredibly loud. He heard a voice pounding down against his brain. *What do you think you're doing,* the voice exclaimed in a low voice. It was an eerie voice; it sounded as if it was spoken on a mountain but somehow was as clear as if someone was standing near speaking to him. It sounded very wise but not quite an intelligent thought. Intelligence requires hard work or hardly working to be more American. The thinkers have no right to call what they do as working; they don't get their hands dirty, they don't bleed or strain their muscles. Everyone knows people make livings off of imagination, but few get recognized for it specifically and the people that do get criticized by other rich people that make livings through being about as creative as a machine with one function. No, this voice was born into wisdom; they were born into intelligence. They created the idea of intellect. Hisako believed he was hearing the voice of God. The idea of God was very strange to Hisako; he never believed he could respect him. *He was born with all that power. He was born perfect but how was "God" born? Whose vagina did he escape?* He never was convinced by the idea of that he simply was. It didn't make sense. Christians use the same argument with evolution. They said so what you're saying is things just happen. It was all just a big boom created from a mixture of chemicals, but where did that come from? Where indeed? Where the fuck did God come from? "God is evolution", Hisako would always joke. Nothing can really explain him and nothing can explain evolution. He had a gut feeling they both sort of existed in a way. He kept most of his theories about the origin of life to himself; he never told his parents for they would worry too much.

'Who are you? ", asked Hisako with a faint stutter in his voice. He already knew the answer but he figured it had a cinematic quality. (Asking the question and everything that is) The owner of the voice exited from the shadows or wherever he was to approach. He did not reply. The apparition just stood there. Hisako or no one could explain what it exactly was, it was only clear that it wasn't from what we call Earth. After about a few minutes of silence, it began to speak. "You are not allowed, according to my laws to travel through timelines and here you are." said the apparition. "Excuse me, you didn't answer my question. Who the hell are you?" insisted Hisako. "I think you know good and well who I am. I am what people of the world call God." replied (well God supposedly). *Well then you can just go to hell.* "Get the hell away from me you bastard", said Hisako. "I can help you", said God. Hisako was pretty astounded seeing something all these years he imagined not real or rather he was not sure it was real. Throughout most of Hisako's life he had been an agnostic. He thought that he might get away with limbo or something if there was a God. "I know what you're thinking and it is not true; you will not go to limbo or Heaven or Hell there is no such places." "There is no reason to get excited", he continued as a way of calming him of this news. "Well what is it them will I be reincarnated?" a confused Hisako responded. "To be honest really you should just rot in the ground", replied God. *Oh shit.* "And you hear to take my life?" he said. "Well no I want you to do it yourself", said god. *No chance in wherever that's happening.* Without thinking, Hisako generated some sort of sharp jabbing device and stabbed God in the chest. *By God, I've killed God.* His dad also had vanished as he had done this. Things were getting too weird for him. *Was his father some incantation of God? Had he really killed God and did that make him God was he God the whole time? Is everyone God but they have some barriers that make them unaware of the fact. He must have killed the authority figure he answered to most. He heard somewhere that God is whatever is most important to you in your life. Maybe that was Jim Morrison, yes, he believed it was.* He wasn't really sure what it meant really. *His father certainly wasn't most important to him but it had been what he groveled to the most. He feared his father most for some reason. Maybe that made him God. What makes god to those that think he is a loving God and wouldn't harm anything?* He didn't want to think of it anymore. He was wondering how the absence of his father would influence the rest of his life in the present. He wondered if it would be much like the **Back to the Future** movies where the smallest changes can make a world of difference. Would this be for better or worse? He suspected there was no one else conscious of God actually existing or this theory of existence. He already had divine powers before he had killed God. *Was it some kind of learned level of consciousness that granted me the abilities, was genetics also a role, and was it the next step of evolution but what a step not possible?* He woke up in his present time only he wasn't in a bar like he was last time he blanked out. He was on the outside of town on a long route stretching seemingly forever. He didn't see civilization anywhere. It was just some freeway that he was walking down. *Why the hell am I on a freeway now? Where should I go? The only place to go is forward.* He was walking down the insane stretch of road and could swear he heard the faint sound of the song **Pissing in a River**, by Patti Smith. "Every move I've made I've made for you" (Patti Smith, 1976) he heard. Who was he moving for; as far as he knew he was his own master was it a victory song for finally taking control of his life? He also heard the question "Should I crawl defeated and gifted?" (Patti Smith, 1976) Did he feel desperate as though he were crawling and defeated despite this great power he had? He came up to a body of water and coincidentally had to urinate. He unzipped his pants and began to in fact piss in the river. It was a strange thing. It felt absurdly religious. The urine added very little to the large body of water really it was only recycled through the body of water that just traveled on and on throughout the world. He zipped up his pants and thought of absolutely nothing (if a psychic were to read him like a one that really was psychic I mean; they would find nothing. It was black as the day the Earth began, if it even began. Maybe it always was. Maybe nothing was made. These very thoughts began to flood his head and then drifted away. He went to the past again and relived his childhood. It felt romantic. He was so fascinated with it. He wanted to see his life without his father as a crutch and make the comparison. When he was finally in the past the experience was forgotten as if he met someone he always wanted as a lover but realized they were not interesting at all in person. Now he saw first bus he had ever seen approach his driveway. It came like a Viking ship. You can make your own connections to the experience; it just fit the moment was all Hisako could think. He couldn't explain it at all.

ᚼISAKO'S ᚑOURNAL

I feel unconnected with it all. With people. With the world. With everything in general. Nothing seems real at all. I feel completely conscious of it somehow. The people say there is a God. I feel absolutely confident one does not exist. I don't say anything, for I know the passion these people have for him. It fascinates me that everyone seems definitely sure that God would be male. I suspected he would be both if one existed. The women don't complain or argue this seemingly definite fact. Oh beggars can't be choosers I guess. This world is dominated by men it seems. The beggars would be shunned and ridiculed. Maybe I should make my own religion up. Perhaps make allot of money off it when I am older. Probably wouldn't happen like I said before, I would get ridiculed for questioning the gender of their God. I guess I'll just sit and listen to them. It's all just noise to me, though. All I can hear is faint humming in a gust of wind and a buzzing in my ears like many locusts singing in unison. The language of people to me is of no more importance to that of animals. I hear the people howl and it sounds as nonsensical as a wolf doing the same. I adopt the human language as my own to avoid being put away. It is funny how I have so much vast knowledge or imagined knowledge of it all and yet I am helpless to question what most call reality. I feel like a God among men and unable to reveal myself.

II

A bus is heading down my road to the residence of my newly adopted mother. I've been orphaned for three years and have received no teaching, so naturally I should be less advanced than the rest of my peers but somehow I feel a change or a doubt. I can't grasp what it is, but I just feel my imagination is either hyperactive or non-existent. I feel as though, I have no need for school as though I know everything that is necessary for me to learn. I vaguely hear my mother say some prayers in the morning to some kind of being, but I don't see anything she is talking to thin air. I don't understand it. She has a look though as if something has changed from how it once was but I've only known her such a short time how could I know what it is. I just feel she has been affected in some way. *Is it because of me?*

The bus approaches the long driveway. I don't understand why our driveway is so long. I have seen other driveways and they are so small their homes are small and what have I done or my family. My mother doesn't even have a husband to help provide; she doesn't even have a job, and somehow we get by. She must have had some kind of husband perhaps he died but how? It feels almost as if this is some kind of alternate reality. I am now getting on the bus.

None of the other children want me to sit by them. They all look at me with confused eyes. I am groomed fairly nice what could be the matter? It probably is an age difference. I am too old to be starting kindergarten. I am around 5 years old. I scout the whole bus for a seat and see a lonesome child in the back slightly younger than myself. He gives me a nodding motion to let me know I can sit there. We started talking about all the cartoons that we watch on television. Most of the cartoons we watched either involved superheroes or talking animals. The entire bus ride to school felt shorter than waiting for the bus to come or even picking a seat (especially picking a seat). I was most alone then. I was so alienated from everyone. It is almost funny that the most alienated student was the most inviting.

As I got to school I realized that I wasn't in kindergarten. I was in 1st grade; my mother didn't want me to appear a giant among smaller kids. Most kids were around my age; most slightly younger. I did see older students outside my classes though. I picked up most things pretty well even with the slight disadvantage of never attending kindergarten. My friend on the bus had the name David Weiner. He talked a little bit about his religion. He was Jewish and so were his parents. It seemed very similar to what my mom believed but their "savior" didn't come yet. He was very genuine about his faith though. He couldn't talk about it intelligently due to him being so young, but I got the idea. I didn't believe it, but I respected him for it. I later learned that people were not very genuine with their religions and that they used them for social status or practiced it once a week and every other day they acted like any other bastard.

I am confused how I automatically seem to have preconceived notions about my future and the actions of people. I can't see people's thoughts but they are easily predictable. I ponder everything on my bus ride home. In my sleep my eyes are wide open I stare into the ceiling with strange obsession and it inspires. It doesn't make sense, but somehow I can't explain any better than that. I study the pattern on the wall but I forget it as quickly as I remember. I am lost in a trance and then suddenly everything turns black.

There is a shard of broken light and as quickly as I see it I am in a city. For some reason I am jogging. I am not myself, or at least I don't feel myself. My thoughts relatively are akin to my own, but they seem more matured and more experienced. I somehow am aware of how I look even when I should be seeing things from a 1st person view. Instead I am looking at myself through 3rd person view and inhabit the same space. I feel older, I don't know how but I do. I am exercising and that is also strange for it is a thing I rarely do of my own will. I am in a place I have never seen. I am strangely very calm and ok with it all. On my jog I encounter someone trying to arrest me, but for some reason they do not have the will to chase after me. The surroundings of this city were beautiful. It looked structurally civilized and advanced but still managed to do it without destruction of much of the wildlife surrounding or inside it. There were trees, flowers and plants all in a city. Even the streets weren't so much of a concrete jungle as I would expect most cities to be. There was grass in various patches. It wasn't ugly like through cracks in the ground they had certain sections for it to specifically grow. The environment was thoroughly a joy to witness; unfortunately it could only be witnessed in the imagination of a mind void of attachments. It was a mind at rest and in a dreamed state but somehow it meant more than only a common dream.

All was well on my jog until I met a stranger along the road. He seemed to know me, but I didn't know him. The man looked slightly overweight or a bit heavier than the standard individual. He had a small beard and a larger mustache that both of which could be visible from a modest length. The man had intensity in his eyes and most times lots of expression in his mouth. He was the kind of person who seemed to grow attached to things and caring about them even when in reality they were quite distant. In a way you could call him very religious, but not in practice. He wasn't a spiritual man by any stretch, but he did have methods to his madness that were rarely based on emotion rather the devotion to the idea of something. In this man's case, it was American capitalism. The man stopped me and spoke to me; he said he was my father. I told him I didn't have one, but I somehow knew he was telling the truth. I had memories that were carried from another life I had. *Was I reincarnated as a bastard child?* It turned out that the man existed in my life, but I never met him; he died prematurely from something that the doctors could not explain. His vast amount of money from corporate banking was inherited to my adopted mother following his death. I continued to question the validity of this dream. *Was it real? It seems all too real but it doesn't make any sense. My memories from times I spent with my father came flooding back into my mind. I was 5 now but in this dream I was a grown man.* My mind was fucked up. I loosely knew the word "fuck" or even heard it. Adults would try to keep these words away from children; it was effective but of course not entirely because they always found out. It was always kind of funny to me how adults swore like drunken sailors but if these same parents saw their children doing it they would just flip.

My father told me that it was I that had killed him. I am not sure this knowledge was to my advantage or not. I always had some sort of feeling in the back of my head it was true, but this put the "icing on the cake" as some would say. This wasn't a mere dream it was an entirely different world and before my very eyes I saw my father fade away. It was not quick. It was slow and gruesome to watch. First his face began to wrinkle more noticeably each second; then parts of his face would peel away behind the layer of skin but he wasn't a skeletal figure underneath he was a spirit or ghost of my father's image. The ghost did the same thing as what was my father until there was nothing left. A great cloud of dust sufficient enough to make up an entire person drifted away. I could see every grain individually; I could somehow give them all names as they flew away from my sight. There was a plate of fruit skins on the ground. It was very strange they were just sitting there. It felt like it was alive in the same way animals and people live, but it was only a fruit and not even the entire fruit either; it was completely devoured. My attention was completely focused on this; there could be an explosion in the background, the whole world could collapse on itself, people could be devoured by their own bodies and I wouldn't shift my attention from these skins. I moved closer to discover the species of fruit. I soon discovered they were peels of mango. I don't understand why this seemed specifically significant. I heard somewhere that mangos were specifically good for the libido. It having to do with sexual activity seemed specifically interesting. Most of the time sex isn't really thought of specifically to bring life, but that is in fact what it does. It is so funny that people get so much pleasure out of sex, but hates their lives. They are connected, but emotions concerning both are very far from each other, and they are not typically thought of in unison or at the same time. Their mind is elsewhere. People can look at life in many different ways, but typically it is boring and mechanical. Grow old, find job, support family and that is it for most people. Some people prepare for death by doing things that please an all-powerful life force that no one can really explain, but they practically beg everyone not to question it for that could jeopardize their chance at receiving paradise. Others try to make the world better or want to and give themselves a way to not some alien being, but a cause that they view as good; they are not religious, but they believe in being "good" whatever that means to them. They are not religious but have some kind of spiritual passion that guides them through life. Others religiously don't question anything about life or the afterlife they just care about themselves and making themselves happy and that is where sex and life intersect, and fly so far from each other. These people go over and above to please themselves and sex almost seems to be the ultimate way of doing it and the cycle continues as they produce children that may take the same path or abstain from their parents ways. While those parents were sweating like greasy pigs the last thing on their mind was the child they would create. My eyes were still focused on the fruit or rather the remains of it, and it seemed to speak to me as a metaphor for life and what was left of it. The world is round; this is a universal fact. This mango was once like the world round but somebody decided to pluck it from a tree or purchase it from a store and sends their teeth tearing into it as their taste buds indulged in the delightful flavor of the tropical fruit. *Was this also the premonition of the state of Earth or the universe? Was it a sign? Was I plucking the fruit metaphorically speaking when I obtain this cosmic perception of the world? This unusual awareness of everything? Could I control my actions? I felt that I had some power but it was not fully realized I felt as if earlier I understood. Everything was so clear but also so confusing. I understood everything yet I also understood nothing.*

The world was falling apart behind me I later realized, as some of my attention was lost from the peel of fruit. There was a terrible man that walked up to me, well he didn't walk he was running in a very clumsy fashion. *Was he handicapped or was he drunk I asked myself.* I knew it was neither of those guesses however and found that the man was wounded. I smelled radiation in the air and some of his skin was peeled off, no doubt from previously mentioned radiation. The man asked me "Why?" I didn't know what to say and next thing I knew I was at the North Pole or someplace similar but I wasn't shivering. It was white everywhere and there was a glowing in the sky. I asked myself in naïve humorous way "Is this Heaven?" I knew it wasn't, but I just thought it would be fun to humor the idea. I later found it wasn't that funny to me. I found another plate buried in the snow and on it was a full mango. *What the hell does this mean?* I closed my eyes and saw two colors in my head, black and white. That's what everything was at the moment. I started blinking and then everything turned gray and then I began to choke. I was gasping for air. I realized now I was lying on the ground. I have no idea how I got there on the ground that is and "to add insult to injury" I was stabbed. There was blood everywhere but it wasn't blood red. It was slowly turning into a reddish color however bit by bit and then I gave my last breath. But that was only a dream.

Hisako's Journal

I woke up from a slumber once I remembered it was the first time. I realized I was living different realities I could not decide on which ones were which. They ended up being all the same to me. It really was the only perspective that really mattered or at least so I imagined. I felt the dream I had altered the future or the present somehow. When I woke I discovered that I was much older. This was surprisingly no shock at all to me. I just wanted to forget everything put it all behind me. Live in a fantasy. That was in the forefront of my mind. I wanted to conform to the institutions and rules as best I could. I just wanted to be like the rest of them; the rest of the people in the world living their mundane boring lives. "No alarms and no surprises", I screamed inside my head. The self-tutoring I thought would be in vain, but it did seem to work for some time. I was 17 and like most any other kid at school somehow I already understood every relation I had with my peers without seeming to have experienced them at all. There seemed to be a shadowy presence there though; it seemed to mock me with the most eerie pleasure. It was all knowing it knew how everything would turn out. It had my heart on a platter. Most nights I would choke on my own fear and shiver it away in my sleep. Everything was completely better in the morning.

III

Hisako woke up for school …. again. This wouldn't be unusual if he had been the same age when he had waked up. He was at least 11 years older than he had been the last day. *Was it really only one day that had past?* Everyone else had acted like nothing had happened; Hisako just went with the flow for his questioning would surely raise suspicion amongst everyone. He acted as if nothing changed. *Did anything change?* He had little to no recollection of the previous day. *Was that part of my dream too?* Many questions went through Hisako's mind but nothing was brought out in the open. His mother waved goodbye as he headed to high school. His father was heading out for work too as he was heading to school. *Wait a minute?* He didn't remember his father being around previous to today. *Was he only on some kind of long trip? Was he lost at sea or something why he wasn't he there?* He didn't remember it was himself that killed his own father; deep down he knew, but he was trying to block it with mental concentration. It was such a large event. One would think killing their father would be something very difficult to forget. His concentration was somehow able to stop it. He got on the bus and it felt very much like déjà vu for he had sat next to the same friend as he did yesterday or what presumably was yesterday. Someone else around them joined in Hisako's conversation with David Weiner. They were two individual's quite different from David. One was a Wiccan girl with the name Cara Klein, and the other was a brainy atheist named Jeff Dallas. They were all good comrades, Hisako thought.

During school Hisako was astounded by how quickly he adapted to the mannerisms of his friends and it felt like he had known them all for a long time. He kept thinking *I just met these people and I know a lot of things about them.* He kept telling himself to shut out these thoughts and live with it as if accepting the way things were was part of some religious calling that he must follow by all costs or their might be great consequences. Jeff Dallas, one of his friends earlier mentioned shared Hisako's interest in comics and video games; in fact they were planned to go Hisako's house after school for the weekend to hang out and play video games. David Weiner would join them to play a lot of the time, but his parents restricted what he could do; he was made to stay home and study most of the time. On few occasions he was allowed to go to friend's houses and his parents always were concerned about what the boy did. David's parents were surprisingly conservative; it was surprising because his family was Jewish and most Jews were left side of the fence. They seemed to carry a devotion to Zionist supremacy of Israel so they supported groups like the ACLJ to insure "God's children" were looked after properly by the United States. It is ironic that America is so focused on preserving Israel when they aren't really supposed to have preferred religions according to the constitution and all that. In addition, America wasn't really a breeding ground for spiritualism, even though it seemed to brag about being looked over specifically by God or at least in George W. Bush's eyes and also many

U.S. presidents in speeches have claimed the United States somehow divinely important. The American capitalist system didn't seem to align with his parents teaching, as well as his churches portrayal of Christ and how he acted. This confused Hisako greatly. America was all about materialism and what made you important was the things that you owned; so many people are hypnotized by flashy ads and commercials. It is all about consumption and seeing how much you can get. Ads for food turn the people to gluttony. Ones for sexual enhancement and phone chat hotlines make them lust. The news and radio make people into hate mongers. Other countries may share in these sins, but America has certainly mastered the craft well. "You make, you buy, and you die! That's the motto of America!" Those were words spoken by a famous rock musician named Joe Strummer of the punk rock band, The Clash. Hisako had recalled listening to those words from a video on YouTube video. He thought of them fondly when he heard his parents banter, or his friend David repeat the banters he heard from his parents about America and capitalism and how goddamned special it was. Hisako knew damn well David's parents supported the conservatives for two reasons.

1. They had Zionist connections and though most Jewish people in the states are liberals; they were very passionate about fighting al Qaeda because they decided to make a target of the Jewish people.
2. They were rich.

David, he knew was just simply brainwashed into his way of thinking; it didn't stop them from being friends however. Jeff Dallas, however, shared a more similar view upon the political spectrum as far as beliefs were concerned. Now Hisako was a fan of capitalism, partially because of his parents and the school's teaching curriculum, but he didn't take it too seriously or at least as much as others had. He knew there were flaws, but he certainly was no bleeding heart liberal, just a normal democrat really. Now Jeff was a bit more radical. He read books by Karl Marx and Fredrick Engels and he was a fan of Malcolm X and Che Guevara and all the radical Marxist people. He liked bands like The Clash, Rage Against the Machine, Anti-Flag, Rise Against, Bad Religion, and the list could go on but he liked allot of punk left leaning alternative bands. So did Hisako, he just didn't take their lyrics as close to the heart. Jeff wasn't really radical though. He could trick people into thinking he was, he knew all the slogans and literature he just didn't have the guts to carry his ideas out. He wanted to start a band and write protest songs but he found out he really wasn't too good at it (even to be in a punk band). He just stuck to reading and playing video games for the time being.

Cara Klein was a different sort of friend; she still had fun with him but it was more of a personal relationship and they talked about their lives at home. While his other friends rarely talked about their own lives apart from school and events they went to; Cara discussed more serious matters. She shared a lot of the same tastes in music as him, much like his other friends. She liked punk bands also but was more into alternative bands with the same ideologies but were not necessarily punk. She liked stuff like Radiohead, Modest Mouse, and R.E.M. She was also into punk bands that David and Jeff didn't necessarily like too much like Patti Smith and Amanda Palmer. Hisako liked those punk bands a lot though and they shared more similar musical tastes really. Cara was different in that she didn't follow a traditional religion or none at all; she was a Wiccan. This interested Hisako a lot but he didn't want to ask about it because he thought it would be embarrassing. She worked at a Burger King; she didn't like it but it was a way of getting money which she didn't value too much really. As her political views are concerned they also fit more closely with Hisako's mold; he cared about things but he felt helpless to do anything about and found everything just pointless. She was a liberal for two reasons.

1. She was judged by her views by conservatives and made to feel bad about her "witchcraft" as they called it.
2. Her parents were also.

As to why her and Hisako never went out on a date was simply they weren't into each other in that way. That was that there was nothing more. It wouldn't be surprising, unless if it was a story to them. Hisako found that much of real life wasn't like any stories on television or movies. People didn't "fall in love" by a simple glance at each other or a few common similarities. As far as he was concerned, everything was triggered by certain lusts that were unique to each person. He didn't really believe in the thing people called love.

It was time for Hisako's gym class; he wasn't particularly fond of that period. Neither were his friends; they often skipped the game they had planned for them. To him and his friends they saw it as childish for 2 reasons; yet again the magic number 2.

1. They were forced to do something just simply because it was a command told by someone older.
2. There was no point to sports in their minds, it was just like tag but with more advanced rules; it was no different to them than Hide and Seek or I Spy or Pin the Tail on the Donkey. The only difference to them is that it made us sweat.

Hisako and his friends mostly only sat in a corner and talked after exercises. Sometimes they poked fun at jocks that seemed to think these sports were so important and cool. We'd say stuff about how wrestlers wore spandex and rolled around with other guys and about them all changing naked in the locker room. It was childish they knew, but they thought jocks were as well. Some of the time, they only did it because they were insecure about their relationship status. Cara had a boyfriend by this time but Hisako, Jeff and David all had never dated and they were sophomores by this time. They would shrug it off and say they had more important things to do than to find dates, which was mostly true but in part it was only an excuse. Hisako wasn't even quite sure he was gay or not to be honest. That is what some kids were telling him at school mostly the jocks actually, but the jocks really seemed most gay of all because he heard stories about how they would bring nerdy weak kids into the locker room and make them show their penis. In addition he saw that they had a strange fascination with grabbing at peoples nipples before a game. He was sure if it was a way to get them pumped up for the game, if it was to annoy people or just plain weird. It was probably at least two of those reasons.

The gym was pretty large, certainly larger a space than we needed just sitting here. Cara and Jake motioned me to a door in the left corner of the gym and I followed. They were smoking pot or at least preparing to at the time; they offered me some I accepted it and "lit up" as some say I guess. It was a good time we laughed and talked about nonsense. Unfortunately, the gym teacher found out *Man was he ugly; I can't believe the man could really teach physical activities properly he must have used videos to show people exercise because he was out of shape. He had like two chins and was very fat. He also taught math; all the students would make fun of him. My friends were guilty of it now. Even as he spotted us and sent us into the principal's office it was hard not to laugh especially when smoking the weed.* It wasn't really embarrassing because of the pot, but it could have been otherwise. Hisako was annoyed with the fact he got in trouble for smoking a bit of weed but "stupid jocks" could get away with harassing girls and trying to breaking their sexual wills. *Most of the girls I am glad to say weren't impressed by these stupid boys at first; some would cave in eventually and the really stupid ones would already be with these boys without them even having to flirt first.* They were in the hallway, Hisako and his friends on the way to the office and suddenly Hisako lost his buzz when he noticed something in the corner of his eye. It was a man or was it a man? In a dark cloak; he looked like the grim reaper. I suppose it is something you could call the creature, but it is very unlikely that humans could figure the identity of the creature by creating the character themselves. A chill up and down Hisako's spine; all his other friends still had buzzes and could not see what Hisako did. He began to think of all the confusion he once had; he drowned it out but it was very hard. It was like some kind of psychic battle between two mystics. This round Hisako won his outer wall was only attacked and some of it crumbled. Now Hisako was at the principal's office along with his friends. Fortunately, the principal was a nice guy and let them off because he knew they were all good students and wanted them to succeed. He didn't want some stupid misdemeanor appearing on their records. The gym teacher would have thrown a fit if he was still in the room. Hisako was thankful and he showed his thanks to the principal and he said "Don't mention it." He was a very casual cool guy. They went to lunch after their office sentence.

It was eating at Hisako, he had to ask Cara about the Wiccan religion; he just wanted to know about the pennants and what they meant or what her religion was all about. He almost considered to perhaps joining in the practice of it.

"Hey, Cara can you tell me about Wicca or whatever it is; it isn't embarrassing that I ask is it?"

"Only if you make it", replied Cara. She started telling him that Wicca was a modern form of Paganism and is defined as witchcraft but some Wiccans including herself don't like to call it witchcraft they like to just call themselves Wiccans. She told him that instead of having a monotheistic God meaning only one God there some Wiccans believed there were two deities. They are traditionally viewed as a horned God and a mother Goddess. This sounded fairer to Hisako than Christianity because both women and men were represented by a powerful being. Cara continued to tell Hisako that these were seen mostly as facets of a greater pantheistic godhead, meaning that instead of a physical figure the whole universe or nature was an all-encompassing "God"; God wasn't merely a person in the sky, but rather made up of everything in the world. Much like Buddhists or Hindus, but it connected more with Hindus for they had actual Godlike figures and many more of them too. This made more sense to Hisako as well; he didn't view God much like some wrinkly old man in the sky with absolute power. It made more sense to have absolute power by inhabiting absolutely everything being one with the whole universe. She also told Hisako of the festivals they had to celebrate eight seasons. They were called Shabbats and she explained those in some detail. Cara was wearing a pentagram necklace and mentioned how the points represented different elements: earth, air, water, wind and spirit. She told him that people had Satanism and Wicca very confused as in Wicca the pentagram symbol the face is pointed upward symbolizing that spirit triumphs over matter while in Satanism they flip the symbol the other way to symbolize earthly gratification. She said she always got annoyed with people thinking she was a Satanist. Cara continued to say that it was difficult being a Wiccan because of the persecution one can receive from people. She mentioned a time when she heard George Bush on the television say Wicca wasn't a religion she got so mad she almost threw something television. She lost many friends because of it she said and that many Christians treated her as a "black sheep" and someone who shouldn't be associated with. They called her a devil worshipper and horrible things of the like. It almost made her want to cut her wrists at certain points but she remembered that part of her ethical code as a Wiccan was to not harm others or her. Hisako was about to ask her about magic and rituals but the next bell rang and they left the table and he said "well that's pretty interesting" and stuff like that.

Hisako was on his way to his next class and he noticed a girl in the hallway that caught his eye. He wasn't so much sexually drawn to her but that was a part of it but he noticed something very strange about her like she was a girlfriend he had had but he didn't remember having any girlfriends in high school yet. Again it must have been something he had done in a past life or something like that. He didn't exactly know what to think. Did he want to pursue her? He decided to ignore the sexual urges he had but it was tugging at him throughout the day. She looked so unusually familiar and he felt that they had already shared some history with each other. She didn't seem to be his type really though; she was rather dull and stupid. Many people would say that she was slut and there was some truth to that statement. Hisako heard her talk about shows like Jersey Shore, Breaking Amish and Duck Dynasty. Hell, all she watched was "reality" television Hisako thought. It embarrassed him that he was so interested in her at first. It was just a real turn off to him.

Hisako's mind was in a daze during his next class. All he was thinking about were Wicca, that girl, and deep, deep inside his mind was the grim reaper specter like character he saw earlier or thought he saw earlier. He didn't know what religion he believed; he believed in something but he couldn't define it really. It seemed that there was something at work aside from just the world but he didn't really think of a specific "God". Maybe "God" was symbolized like the Wiccan deities in the way a Queen represents England but didn't really do anything herself. The world he imagined was all one everything connected like the universe was all a part of everything. He started to wish he had sexual feelings toward Cara;

she was such a good friend and she was smart. He thought she could put these confusing things he had in his head in perspective and also fuck her too. He hated being attracted to that other girl; she was so stupid he couldn't believe it. She was the kind that obsessed over celebrities and what people thought of her. He wished she was dead all of a sudden because he had this feeling he would defile his body someday by having sex with a stupid whore like that. He would be married to some broad who hated him and he hated her but not her looks and would get sick of love making very shortly after a few goes. He never thought of the kids or that she would someday lose her appearance but he still imagined a terrible life regardless. Who was the specter he saw before it tugged and tugged on his brain. He got so upset that he pounded on his desk and the teacher looked up to see what the matter was but he didn't answer. The teacher didn't care anyway he just asked because he knew he was supposed to. Hisako could swear he heard screaming and rumbling in the distance but not enough of a feeling to call much attention to it. The bell rang and he was gone the first to leave the room.

The final hour of his school day passed and he was on his way home. He didn't take the bus; he hated the bus.

His mother called his cell phone. "On your way to work?" the text message read.

Hisako didn't even know he had a job. He was worried to ask because for who didn't know the place they had worked? Luckily, as he passed a convenience store a friendly voice asked, "Hey, Hisako do you work today?"

I assumed that was my place of work and I replied, "Yeah". I went into the workplace and found out I was a stock person and started work right away. I clocked in and did what I figured I was supposed to do and it came pretty natural for I must have done it before. I didn't remember but I was conscience of the activity. If I thought real intent I knew that I had had 2 or 3 previous lives to one I had now. I shared all the capabilities of myself in those lives in addition to what I am learning now it made me very capable in school work so I could focus on other things. I was really pretty average as far as IQ is concerned, but I found really I was quite brilliant for I shared a few other minds than my current one. This realization became fantastic to me as it was curse before due to the confusion, but I was learning to come to terms with it as I stocked the shelves. *This is a gift not a curse I thought. I can make life good for myself that is all I need to worry about; myself. If I only focus on myself I can make life good. If I think too much I'll go nuts, but if I use the combined knowledge of my past lives I can use the experience to get ahead.* Capitalism actually looked good for Hisako, but really he had an unfair advantage than the rest in his life. Maybe his plans may not be so successful. Everything would have to just make its way around the bend.

Hisako's Journal

Things were looking up for me on my spiritual quest within myself. Everything wasn't cloudy anymore. Almost as if I could see a future for myself as to previous it was unimaginable or dismal. I wanted to see if I could prove my previous conceptions false and be a very successful individual, I figured I could probably become a manager with enough effort. I never before wanted to pursue a job in corporate business, but I thought that really it is one of the easiest ways to become successful. I saw it as selling myself to a hypothetical devil before, but as long as I make a living I thought what the hell. My early attempts were in vain I assumed because I figured I must have done something wrong before to have to repeat my life again. Or am I just repeating the same mistakes? What the hell. It just feels right for me. I am filling with confidence. Everything feels clear.

IV

I woke up to a weekend and I was to head to work again for most of the day. As I got up from bed I made a big stretch and yawn; it was done in a very animated way, like in a cartoon or something. In fact I could swear I heard a rooster screech as I woke from my rest. I felt positive about the day, I wasn't usually a morning person, but today was an exception to that rule. I had found more purpose in life than I have in a long time. I headed to the restroom and brushed my teeth and took a shower; everything was in its right place. It was almost eerie how cliché the events seemed to be in my head; everything was played out perfectly they weren't difficult tasks but it didn't trip even a little on my way to anything. I didn't drop soap, I brushed without any kind of distraction, I made my eggs perfectly for breakfast and I must have showered really well because I smelled and looked just great! It was fortunate that work was not very far away because I didn't have a car yet. I took all the things I needed: A polo shirt, jeans and my badge to clock in. I wasn't very tired when I clocked in probably because I had a good night sleep the day before. I met my manager for the first time or at least in this reality or life. My boss seemed pretty nice to add to my so far great day. His name was Mike Farnaby.

If I was reincarnated then my boss probably wouldn't be the same, but no it couldn't be reincarnation because my mom was the same from my last reality I lived. I definitely ruled two things out in my pursuit of answers. I didn't believe in a monotheistic religion or reincarnation. I can see my future and beginning in fractured pieces, but I have never seen any kind of visible "God" figure and I ruled out reincarnation just now. It's unlikely everyone would end up in the same place in my life again and would look the same most likely either. I was open to the idea of pantheism, the belief that "God" instead on a guy in the sky was more like inside everything. While thinking slightly upon this, I continued with my brain numbing job.

The stock person job was so easy I had to consistently think of things to do or think of things in general while I worked. Even then it still was taking a toll on my mind because of the mechanical routine of it all. I wasn't trapped behind a register, but I still felt trapped and alienated from my superiors. I didn't talk very much in addition to thinking, but when I did talk it felt like such a great activity to partake in I would like to just bullshit talk about politics. I hardly knew what I was saying and I knew half of what I said it was like I got the basic concept of what I said, but not the specifics so much. Some people talked with me others nodded off. Mike was one of the people that made good conversation. He seemed pretty reasonable; if I were to guess, I would say the man was an independent. He also could be a registered democrat with a blend of liberal and conservative views. I remember he had a theory things would go good for the country if for 1 term we had a democrat and the next a republican. I agreed in a sense I thought that way nothing brilliant would happen but things would be fairly decent. Mike's vision was almost how things were really only most of the time the president would go through 2 terms because of the great advantage in campaign funds they would have for the next election. It was no surprise and very predictable when Obama won against Romney. Not just because Romney lied left and right and anyone with a brain stem should see through it but also despite Romney's large wealth and big business backers the presidency offers too much an advantage when money is concerned that nothing could threaten it unless the president were to do some blatant stupid thing, but even then George Bush got elected for two terms, but there was voter fraud. I hope that is the reason anyway that he was elected twice; that and money but the people certainly didn't vote for him.

Mike was a catholic and of I'm guessing of Irish descent. His hair was dark blond and he was balding in the back of his head. I had a strange connection with the Irish people I think. Every Irish person I've met or most of them I've connected pretty well with. It probably is a big coincidence but I couldn't help but to think of it. Most of them I've met have been a mix of an inviting kindness but not overboard with it. Hisako would only talk to Mike on his lunch breaks at work and by around closing time when there was nothing really to do. Aside from their work life they never met each other after work or anything; it would be weird if they had for the great age difference. If it had not been weird like that, Hisako could envision them being good friends.

Hisako had good relations outside of just Mike, but Mike was the only person he would frequently talk to. In fact, Hisako hardly knew the names of anyone else that worked with him but he had good relations with them.

He was nice to them and they were nice to him. The girls he worked with ranged from fairly good looking to sometimes not at all good to look at. Hisako's dad would always be an ass and nudge him a certain way when he eyed a good mate in his opinion for Hisako. It was like a twisted backwards version of Romeo and Juliet, Hisako thought. He wasn't in "love" with anyone, but his parents would want to pair him up with other people. *They're both probably worried about me turning out to become a homosexual.* He almost wishes that he was to only spite them. In fact he did, he wanted nothing more to see the look on his father's face when he had heard the news. He imagined that his father would over react and spout of maybe try and take a swing at him and would end up committing suicide. As for his mother he suspected she would get a bit upset and when her husband committed suicide she would weep for hours most nights. This was a sadistically joyful vision for Hisako. Not much would please him more. How terrible it was that he wasn't gay he thought.

"Hisako to produce to fill", the announcing speaker called aloud. He made his way over to the cooler. It was near the cosmetics section of the store. The girl at the cosmetics counter gazed at Hisako with lustful eyes. Lusts not love; Hisako didn't know love he didn't think it existed. She walked closer to stock some shampoo which also was in the same section as the cosmetics; she only partly did it for duty, but mostly to just get closer. Hisako looked over for a second and she made a motion to the restroom and he got slightly turned on. After he was done stocking the produce; he made his way over there. Something was strange to him about the whole situation, because he had never been with a girl or felt any were in anyway attracted to him. He was thinking what the heck most of the time, but the ringing of his parents stupid cautioning about "no sex before marriage" was in his ears. He wanted to ignore it, but it was so fucking hard for him to do it. Before he knew it he was almost there with the girl and everything, but as they were about to grope each other; he refused the invitation and left. After he did it he wondered what the hell he was doing, but then again he was also wondering what else he could do. If he got this girl pregnant; could he raise a family, would he even like her after that experience, did they even have much in common aside from the lust towards each other at the precise moment? He had too much respect for women to just get them pregnant and leave them. He didn't respect them in the stupid traditional gentlemanly way that people follow because they are told to be especially gentle to women and treat them as more and somewhat lesser creatures as well at the same time. He respected them in a different type of way; he didn't want to be a womanizing meathead that never commit to their lover. After that movement she made no advances. She either thought he was homosexual or had snotty superior attitude about him. She didn't show any interest any other time around him nor did he her.

Hours passed and it was time for Hisako to clock out. He was supposed to meet Jeff for a movie later and then go to his house afterwards to play video games for a bit and then go back home. They went to see some dumb horror movie. They always liked to watch horror movies and knew they usually weren't that great, but this one really sucked in both their opinions. It made Hisako almost depressed to have wasted so much money to see it. On the way back to Jake's house they continued to talk about how stupid the story was and the characters and the lousy nod to another sequel at the end. They quit their talking for a while and played some Call of Duty. After that they talked for a bit about their parents.

"What makes you most annoyed with your parents?" Hisako asked.

Jeff answered that it was how conservative his parents were. He said, "My dad still thinks Bush was a great president after his last term and thinks Bill Clinton somehow was more responsible for the debt of our country instead of Bush."

"HaHaHaHa!" they both laughed about it. Hisako added, "My dad voted for John McCain only because of that dumb broad Sarah Palin."

They both laughed again. "Really?" Jeff asked still chuckling a bit. "Yep", Hisako nodded.

They grabbed a few beers and started drinking a little bit. They weren't obnoxious drinkers; just casual ones.

"Maybe your dad has the hots for her", Jeff added. He was a third joking but he was closer to the truth than he ever imagined really.

They both had another good laugh. They both sighed with much enjoyment like two middle aged men remembering themselves in their youth and all the time they had before they had grown old only they weren't old. They talked a bit about their confusion that their parents thought Barack Obama was some Big Brother from 1984. They thought he was a socialist dictator; like the talk shows would religiously preach this theory day and night. In reality, they thought he was rather shy on his liberal sensibilities; that or the congress and senate would block any efforts for him to do so. They thought it was annoying when they blamed Obama for drone killing when President Bush allowed these things under the US Patriot Act which was the only Big Brother thing about Obama really; the fact he was continuing Bush's policy and keeping that act. It was harder to get mad at Obama because the republicans were so double standard about it; they talked about Obama being Big Brother with looking into privacy and using drones but if Bush did it they said it was to protect the country or the good of the nation or some shit.

They sighed again, in much the same way as before. Jeff asked Hisako why he believed in God and Hisako reassured Jeff that he actually didn't or wasn't sure. "Oh" Jeff replied in a sort of surprised way. He talked about how Hisako used to be real religious.

Now Hisako was even more confused. He could remember himself being neither conservative nor religious. He always thought he was moderately liberal and agnostic his whole life. Jeff told him about how he used to read stuff from Rush Limbaugh and bring it to school. If Hisako really tried he remembered that he had done it in another timeline. To Hisako, this timeline that faded were no different than days in someone's life. In a way he was immortal and kept starting back at the age of one. Life just kept going on. *Was it the same for other people?* Hisako asked Jeff if he remembered himself being some kind of age that he hadn't gotten to yet. Jeff gave Hisako an obviously puzzled look.

"What the hell are you talking about?" Jeff asked.

Hisako told Jeff about how he kept having "dreams" of times him was older than he was now but they seemed to be more ancient times. He told him he had a cosmic awareness not of a religious godlike being but some kind of idea how the world was made.

"Hmm I don't know; my opinion is that it's all in your head." "Eh, you're probably right." Hisako only agreed because it was an awkward conversation he didn't want to continue, but he knew damn well it wasn't only his imagination.

"Why don't we call it a night?" Jeff said.

Hisako replied, "That sounds great; see you at school in few days."

He walked out his house and took a brisk walk down the road and looked at the town in which he lived. He didn't know whether to look fondly upon it or in hatred. It seemed a very happy town, not too prosperous but a few businesses were there. A gas station, dinner, a pizzeria, a bank, a church and the convenience store in which he worked, but that was about it; all the other places had been closed down. There was some construction for a Dollar General. The lack of prosperity could be blamed on the Sam's Club just outside the town along the way the more city-like area. He stopped inside the diner to grab a bite to eat. Come to think of it; he never really went into the diner that much, or at all in this lifetime. The waitress was loud and obnoxious; she was friendly but an annoying folky kind of friendly. Some customers she chatted with especially, since they were frequent customers. It took a long time for the waitress to focus any attention on him she was just chatting away. Hisako stared intently at her lips while talking to the frequenter; they seemed to be moving unusually slow. Tension was building in Hisako's head; he was losing patience. In reality, it wasn't too long, but the special attention given to other customers kind of disgusted him in a way. He didn't know why; it was just bothering him quite a bit. The roof of the establishment was in need of repair. You could see some cracks in the ceiling with some water dripping down from them. As Hisako was admiring the lousy ceiling, his waitress finally made her way to his table and asked

"May I take your order" with a friendly smile but not as friendly as the others she asked.

"I'll just have a meatloaf sandwich."

"Any sides with that", she asked.

"No, I only want the sandwich and some water."

"All righty" the waitress said with a somewhat annoyed voice. "It will be done shortly", she assured him.

She headed back to the kitchen and the ceiling was creaking even more. You could almost hear it. And then suddenly without warning; it collapsed right behind a short old man that the waitress would call Mr. Magoo. The waitress started laughing because the man didn't move or even seem to notice that the roof fell. She howled in laughter; it was very obnoxious. It took her a while to even acknowledge the mess had even been there. There was water all over the floor; it was all the water leaking from the ceiling. She didn't tell anyone to get a mop or anything; she just stood there laughing. Hisako could believe it. It was just astounding to him. *Well, when you are going to clean it up you fucking bitch!*

After maybe 5 minutes of comments and laughter directed at "Mr. Magoo" she noticed the water and said "Ok, I'll get that cleaned up."

Hisako was thinking about the whole thing until he got his sandwich. He paid and left as soon as he could; he couldn't be out of there faster. It was really depressing for him; it made him think of how inevitable existence was or trying to earn money and make a business or be a part of one. The diner was a lousy one and it wasn't a very good business but what really made it all that much better than any other. There was the difference in income, but what could money buy you just more things to indulge in. Hisako didn't really understand what else there was to find in life but passions and objects. Living in an American capitalist society all his life had something to do with it surely. The people in the diner were so uninteresting; they didn't think about anything outside what they did. They weren't particularly selfish, but they just didn't put any thought into if there was an afterlife, or what the government did. He envied them; their ability not to think about anything. They were oblivious to worry. They believed in God or said they did but they never thought about him. They never thought about the people God allowed Samson to kill after he disobeyed God and asked him for forgiveness if he could destroy his enemies. They forgot Sodom and Gomorrah and the divine judgment he hypothetically made upon the cities for their great "sins" of sodomy, or the King David, who was supposedly a man after God's heart but he had been a really terrible man if you actually read the Bible. He was guilty of adultery with a woman named Bathsheba and tried covering up the pregnancy and killed her husband when he couldn't. Hisako could never imagine himself doing such evil things but a man that was considered so holy and great was guilty if he even had existed. Those people didn't think about the horrible damage Christianity had done on the world. The knights Templar during the crusades and the killing they did in the name of Christ. People liked to think of God as a loving God, but history proved again and again that he was not or at least those that followed him did not love; they were blind to the history and bought the lies they told themselves. They somehow thought that Christians never were anything but a peaceful community of people and somehow thought if anyone was persecuted it was them. They couldn't be farther from the truth. Never, throughout my life have I seen a Christian persecuted for their faith, Hisako thought. David was bullied plenty by other for being Jewish as well as Cara for her Wiccan beliefs and even Jeff for being an atheist was harassed by some adults. It hurt Hisako deeply to think and question it. He tried to forget it and made his way home.

Hisako came home and sat in his bed; he stared up at the ceiling and had a look on his face as if he were about to raise his hands in the air scream and ask the hypothetical heavens "Why was I born, why was anyone made?" He grabbed some of his dad's beer from his private cooler and drank himself to sleep. During his sleep he was seeing a faint orange ray of light, he moved closer to it and could hear crickets or locusts or perhaps the buzzing of the sun's rays. It could be anything at this point, he was only unconscious. It could be the faint sound of any of those outside, his consciousness making psychic interaction in an unconscious state. There was a howling noise and he didn't only see blackness beyond the faint orange light. It sounded like it was coming from the outside of his house's door. He went down stairs to see what it was and to his surprise it was a wolf at the door. He shut the door immediately and hid behind it. The wolf was not strong enough to break the door down, but it did not leave. Instead it faded into a mist that was hardly visible and phased through and became the image of a man about the age of 50 give or take a few years. He had many wrinkles but his physique was splendid. Hisako didn't think he was handsome in fact there was something underlying in his appearance that made him horrifying. His face was a grayish color but his voice was very romantic and charming. Then Hisako thought *is this man a vampire?* Hisako couldn't make any of the man's words out; he could only remember the distinct sound of his voice. He had the idea that the two had met but they definitely had not. Of course he wasn't real, since it was an imagined projection from his unconscious mind. The man had a hypnotic influence over what Hisako did. In fact, before Hisako knew it he was on his hands and knees stacking shelves in a store for some reason. In reality he was stacking blocks at home that his parents kept from when he was a child who used to play with such things. He was in the store; he was employed at. *Was this all symbolic?* Hisako thought. Before he knew what was happening, the girl who had tried seducing him earlier at work slapped him in the face. He began to trip and then trip again. He was tripping as if it were going out of style or in style. He just couldn't stop. He tried crawling away but something kept him glued to the ground. Not anything physical but maybe mystical or telekinetic. Slimy gastropods slithered all along his body and he cried out and broke free from his limitations. He jumped and it seemed like a whole minute before he made contact with the ground. While in the air, he couldn't hear any noises at all. He couldn't see much either, just the dizzying view of the ceiling going up and down and spinning around but he finally made it to the ground and sudden everyone was still and all was quiet. Then, suddenly a horrible squawking made itself present. It sounded like a bird and it was. It was stuck up above somewhere in the lobby of the store. It persisted in its annoying noises, never straining tone or volume. The voice from the bird began to sound human.

It said, "Going down". "Going down, Going down, and Going down." It continued in a sequence of threes.

This sequence lasted 18 times and then someone from inside the store shot the bird with a rifle. It fell to the ground and he shot it twice more for the bird didn't die after the first shot, or even as it descent onto the ground from the great height in which it fell. Hisako gasped, fell on the ground, and cried for some time. He looked up and noticed he was back in his kitchen and he eyed the knives. They lay upon a cutting board next to a scented candle; it didn't smell like anything or at least anything distinct. The candle was supposed to have a distinct scent, but it didn't match the apple pie it said on the label. He kept staring upon the knife, and before he knew it he was at the cutting board holding the knife. He took it and made an incision in his wrist and scratching was heard by his door. He stopped what he was doing to let it in; it was a cat. It rubbed against him and lapped up the blood that dripped from his wrists that fell on the ground. It came from his wrist into the air and then upon the ground, the cat licked the blood, savored it and the let it digest, Hisako raised the knife, slit his wrists and yelled. This cycle went on for some time and Hisako fell to the ground probably from exhaustion from losing so much blood. He lay by the cupboards, and the cat lay atop his lap licking his wounds. Hisako used the remaining of his energy to give sobbing noises and his glands created the tears to give the sobbing some company. The cat sat there rubbing against him. In reality he lay there in the same position with the cat by his side drinking the blood on the ground. His parents woke up and were surprised to witness the scene.

Buzzing filled the cadence for just a little while as the life faded out of Hisako's eyes. The theoretical light at the end of the tunnel was growing dim but that turned out to actually be the light of the sun fading as he closed his eyes. In a state of unconsciousness he saw an orange dot in his sleep or was he sleeping it was hard to tell it felt like little to no time had passed since the time between the fatal wounds and this strange new world of dreams. *Dreams beyond the grave perhaps?* No, it wasn't like that. As shortly he woke to see the fading sun arrive once more to his vision but this time it was throw the glass window up by the ceiling. The ceiling not of his house but of his workplace; it was quite odd it very much felt like he had dozed off for a second, but in that second much activity had happened and he tried briefly to discover when he had first closed his eyes before the obscure dreams and then the strange thought came to him that they were more than dreams. He shrugged it off and texted his Jeff on his cellphone asking if they wanted to see a film later. He wasn't allowed to have his phone out at working whilst working, but he didn't care or respect work so much anymore. He didn't see any benefit coming to him at this place and he felt no pride working there it was only brain dead tasks you were expected to complete. Despite how individualist he tried to make the job by not following a list and just spontaneously finding new things to do every second ultimately he was still working for the corporation and also was dependent on them paying him. The people who did the "real" work lived outside America in sweat shops he would position all these things in this store. Much of the produce and meats would go bad and be wasted when no one bought them. Genetic manipulation and production and deregulation of the activities concerned allowed for bad, but various products that had several of previously mentioned products go to waste. It was disgusting for Hisako to think of aiding in the selling of these manufactured products, this manufactured sickness. *Oh well he sighed and thought maybe someday I'll get a break.*

Hisako (a few moments later) got a response on his phone saying that he would be picked up to see the movie. He told his parents that he would be out later and that they didn't need to pick him up from work. Movies were a casual pleasure that Hisako invited when he felt there wasn't much to do. In reality despite all the stores and things there wasn't much to do; he didn't possess vast amounts of money. Even if he did, how many things would he want to buy? Many of the things he did buy were not consumable things, so there was really no need to get so many items because he wasn't quite finished enjoying the sustainable items he owned. By sustainable that meant items he could enjoy for a long time without having to throw it out or lose interest. He bought books and cds and you could read the same book a few times and not fully grasp its enjoyment and that goes the same with music. There are different moods one has whilst enjoying both things that the effects of both might change depending on the situations in which they choose to experience them. Yes, the only activities that Hisako realized he had been doing with his friends were seeing movies, bowling, and eating out somewhere. The best thing he wanted to do in truth was simply talking about things heavy on his mind like politics and philosophy. He never connected with many people through these constant questions tugging on his mind. It was like he would have to sneak these things into a conversation when they seemed related. He hardly understood what most people talked about, he figured many talked about relationships, but he never really had a real relationship not even a true friend. He seemed to have some acquaintances that enjoyed each other's company, but in the sense of someone that would always be by your side through thick and thin seemed so distant to him and he imagined very few people in America had this kind of relationship. It seemed to him that people were expected to enjoy several quick fast paced social relations and act as though these were deep commitments. The individual was said to be to be praised, but their felt this ridiculous sense of bureaucracy without any comradery. If the workers controlled the business or industry he suspected there wouldn't be the same problem of shallow relations. It was said this kind of thing was impossible. That some higher being must oversee the worker's activities and a few people would control the wages. Also it was understood somehow that higher profits to the top meant the same for the bottom, that they were working together somehow, but of course people realized the inequality of wages. They would defend themselves by saying they deserved more because their work was more mentally demanding. I couldn't imagine how really it just sounded very time consuming, boring and unsatisfying so I didn't intend to pursue any path such as that. I couldn't really argue that point they have the money because they sold their soul and chose profit over themselves. A business I think is about the least artistic activity one can commit to and therefore making it the least human. The goal of it is to keep your employees and consumers happy whilst keeping your profits up. The way this happened now was depending on the labor of others in third world markets and having "democracy" brought to these places and jobs for the people and these markets were the most "free" in the world according to libertarian rights point of view because the workers could not regulate anything and neither could they force the government to. The industry in other countries was savage to the workers who lived there and this is how the products were so cheap. They made allot of things without paying the workers a good wage for the long hours put in, the conditions were not important to them and needed not the fixing up. To label it "free trade" sounds ridiculous if you really study what happens, it is only free for the elites and the elite's job was to make the poor stay there and not challenge the authority.

Before he knew it his friends were there to pick him up. His friends were pretty excited to see another horror movie (these were movies his friends regularly enjoyed) but Hisako seemed disconnected from his friends at the moment. They were enjoying pleasant conversation amongst each other and Hisako would occasionally humor some of the jokes the group would tell by chuckling. To tell the truth it was hard for him to determine when he enjoyed their company and when he pretended to. Most of the time it seemed like that these feelings collided and played off of each other and would trick him into legitimately thinking the company he had was enjoyed. It seemed like on all accounts he over dramatized his enjoyment, but he enjoyed himself all the same.

They entered the cinema and got their popcorn and drinks and went into the theater. The movie was pretty short, but sometime during the movie he sort of dozed off and forgot much of what the film was even about. After the movie was over Jeff drove Hisako to work and went away the others to get a drink. Hisako became confused as he thought he had just been to work, but realized during the movie he had fallen asleep and figured it must have been another one of his dreams. It was odd though for it felt like such a real dream and it made him even questions the reality of his own current existence. Hisako was annoyed that he had to work; he had allot on his mind. He was more attracted to Cara than before even in a more sexual way. He didn't want these feeling he wanted to respect her relationship with her boyfriend, Dave and they had such a great friendship; he didn't want these thoughts to get in the way of it. He thought of the voice in his head. *Did the creature die he thought; is it all over? Is it fucking finally done?* He really liked this thought; he didn't want to be pestered by all these things. He only wanted to have a "normal" life. Deep down in his gut though he knew there were still things happening; he felt his skin tingle. It was like his whole body was asleep for a second. He didn't like it not one bit. He kept thinking; before he knew it he was doing mundane tasks as he was thinking. He had already been on the clock and working for the clampdown. *Will I always be in this place?*

HISAKO'S JOURNAL

I woke up that morning with the sun shining directly in my face, my parents screaming and myself sighing in thirds: agony, confusion, and from just being plain tired. I wish my parents didn't scream as much as they did. It made my head ache throughout the day. The Sunday church service didn't make it much better. To add to that today I was seeing all kinds of strange things throughout the day. I couldn't hold back the images and the consciousness of the universe any longer.

V

"What did you do?" Hisako's mother asked.

"I honestly don't know." Hisako answered. "Why are your wrists cut; you some kind of wimp?" Hisako's dad asked.

Hisako shrugged the minor insult to his masculinity off and said nothing. "Just don't make a big deal out of this; I'll clean up the blood mom."

"Oh ok get some bandages for your hands though." Hisako nodded in agreement. That was the end of it. Hisako couldn't believe it; he would have expected his mother blabbing about the situation to some people after the thing happened.

"Well it's time to go to church", Hisako's mom said.

"And it's time for me to go to work" said his dad.

Hisako made a sigh. He was annoyed about going to church because he hated church and his dad trying to sound like "the big man" of the family. *Yes, it was up to him to put bread on the table and bring home the bacon as some say.*

This was all very strange, the whole situation just a few moments ago he was at work he thought but he must have been nodding off in his sleep as he lost consciousness from the self-inflicted pain he had caused upon himself. Was it a dream? Was it real somewhere else? Are dreams reality? It did not matter much at all now he was all fine and healed up and was on his way to get ready for church. People may say that young children are most easily influenced but this simply wasn't true for Hisako, he remembered when he was a kid going to church no one could keep him interested in the sermon almost as if he knew it was useless information but as it was drilled into the brain and on through school he was indoctrinated in it all but coming of age into the years of a young adult he started again questioning the legitimacy of the dogmas and doctrine.

Hisako began to be bothered that he had to follow his parents everywhere they went or most places. He didn't have a car of his own so he had to ask permission to use theirs or rely on other friends that had cars of their own to drive him places. It made him feel so trapped; the only places he was guaranteed access by himself were work and his house. His mom went out to her car and turned on a Christian radio station which further annoyed Hisako; he hated Christian rock. It seemed really fake to him. The lyrics for the most part he thought sounded not very passionate. He thought it was like mindless chanting mostly and they just said stuff like "God is good, God is strong" and stuff like that. He couldn't relate to it at all. He questioned about God much, but he never thought he seemed powerful or concerned about anything. People he heard would say defending Christianity would say the Earth must have a creator because it is in such perfect order; he didn't see how the world was in order at all. They try to explain the problems through Adam who ate the fruit on the tree that God told him not to eat. He was tempted by his partner Eve and she was tempted by Satan. Why keep Satan around to tempt people? He cast him out of Heaven to know that later he would ruin the planet he made? It just didn't make sense and it never did. As far as Hisako was concerned God was an asshole, even worse than Satan really. In even further beginning God was in Heaven with all his angels and one named Lucifer didn't like God being king and almighty ruler of everything; so what did God do? He threw him down into eternal torment. God doesn't want anyone thinking for themselves, but yet he tries to claim that he does by giving people the right to choose but when they do it wrong they get punished so he basically wants everyone to not think in the end and wants everyone to look fondly on him and bow down and praise him. "Oh halleluiah is the Lord God Almighty." He wants to hear that in the end chanted over and over again. It made Hisako sick to think about it if the hypothetical religious theory had been true.

"Here we are", said Hisako's mom as the car came to a halt in the parking lot. It wasn't parked very straight. Hisako's dad would make stupid comments about it implying that women can't drive and so on. As Hisako went into church he felt very alone. He wasn't friends with any of the kids. He had only three friends and none of them were Christians. Old people held out their hands to shake his as they passed out unneeded bulletins. *It was always the same routine in church; announcements, some songs, greeting people, offering and the sermon.* He just didn't get the destruction of some trees to make these pamphlets. All the people at church weren't genuine; they all tried acting nice but it wasn't a genuine kindness. It was like I'm being nice because I don't want to burn in hell, and if I find out that doesn't matter I want someone coming down with me. Hisako saw his mom chatting away with some lady who Hisako always found strange. He didn't know why there was always something odd about her. How she always lifts her arms during songs and would shout amen very loud after the pastor said certain things.

She seemed to think God was really there unlike most people that just obviously hoped there was but said they 100% believed him anyway. She seemed to be possessed or something. Religious leaders of old would probably say she had demons and would whip her. Thinking about all these things made the time pass rather quickly up until the sermon; of which he like to pay some attention to see if it was full of crap or something to think about.

The pastor came up to the podium; with humble grace for a religious person. I gave this man a chance because he didn't seem so pious and a lot of the time he had some good things to say. Today he started talking about salvation which is one of those things you hear about a million times but don't really understand it fully at all. I listened in to see if any of it made sense. He started talking about the Catholics and how he said they thought they could buy their way to Heaven. He remembered his parents said they were Catholics once and they didn't like it; they became Protestants. I've met a few Catholics and they seemed like fine people to me, but this man seemed to be saying that these nice good people who believed in Jesus and all that would go to hell even when they followed the teachings of Jesus and all that. I can't say I've met as many nice Protestants as Catholics. Protestants were obsessed with money. I learned it in my sociology class that Protestants resented the Catholic idea that going to church and following scripture would get you saved and they said you just had to wait until you die to find out where soul goes. Then they made up a phony idea that money was blessing from God so if you are pleasing God you will get money. This made all Protestant people focused on getting money and holding on to it; I found this odd, Jesus talked about aiding the poor I believe. The protestant sect left a bad taste in my mouth. They said though that if you accept Jesus as your savior you are guaranteed for Heaven. I'm sure the Catholics had the same routine of accepting Jesus and all that. So how come they weren't able to go to Heaven I thought. He talked about how Catholics ask for forgiveness is the wrong way; he proceeded to say a priest isn't necessary to deliver people from sins and that you just have to ask God yourself. I really never understood praying to God; if you really trust him why would you have to ask for anything. It always seemed selfish to me in a way. If Jesus Christ died for everyone's sins why do people even have to ask for forgiveness; that was what the pastor tried making clear but he proceeded to say that you must absolutely by all circumstances keep in God's word. I thought *if you're already forgiven why do you have to keep trying to show God you're an upstanding; you are forgiven?* It wasn't like I was thinking just because you were saved you had all this freedom that you can sin all you want, but how committed exactly did they want you. They never gave a definite answer what living your life for Jesus was. *Is it being simply following his way? Or being obsessed with scriptures? Did you have to go out and preach for your entire life? What the fuck does Jesus want from us?* He kept saying Jesus wanted nothing your sins are already paid for them talked about all these things you needed to do. There was no certainty in salvation; he couldn't admit it or tell the truth about it. He also couldn't really prove God or Jesus existed. I had to just leave the building I made soft sigh and got out of the place as fast as I could without disrupting the other church goers.

I sat down on a park bench outside the church watching cars, trucks and occasional motorcycles drive by. I opened a pack of cigarettes that I had and put one in my mouth and without using my hands to finger it out of the pack; I just took it out with my teeth. I lit up and just started thinking. I was thinking but if you were to visualize my thoughts you wouldn't see much anything. There was too much clouding my head really. I thought about my past and my future simultaneously. They crossed seeming one in the same. I continued to just stare at the town and noticed something that caught my eye. Behind a sort of strip mall (it was just some buildings next to each other of all these different local businesses) it was like this town's excuse for a mall or industry. It was this figure moving very quickly; it came outside their back window and jumped over a fence and I'm presuming went down the alleyways. The figure wore a black hood and my eyes may be deceiving me but it had these horns very much like a bull. It had a body like a man though. I thought *Is this the horned deity from the Wiccan faith?* Before my next thought about the matter my mom touched my shoulder and I turned towards her as she did this. She had an upset look on her face. I thought of two reasons she might be upset.

1. She never knew I smoked and caught me with a cigarette in my mouth.
2. I abruptly left church.

I happened to be correct on both accounts.

She asked me to stop smoking she said, "Get that cigarette out of your mouth before I shove it down your throat." She said it in a nice way; she wasn't literal in her threat, she just wanted me to stop was all.

I took the cigarette out and stuck it in the stone ash tray they had by the bench.

"What's the matter honey", she said.

I replied nothing.

She didn't buy it even when it was true; she had this thing where there always had to be a problem when I sat alone. My mom continued to question me and I said something like I don't believe in God anymore even when I hadn't for some time and it really wasn't a problem. I felt absolutely fine but she didn't believe I was fine. It was like you need Jesus's help to be happy. No, I thought; there are perfectly happy atheists out there as well as there are very miserable Christians in the world. We have had talk before about me questioning God's existence and all that but I was real up front with it this time.

I just said "I really don't believe in it." "I hate religion", I said; "it only creates problems in the world", I continued. "Even in today's message us Protestants are trying to get these people down on Catholics; I've met some very good Catholic people and them damning them like that just makes me so angry." My mom tried to calm me down but I was too fired up. I said how the Protestants were hypocrites following Jesus but going against him on the help the poor thing; I explained Max Weber's findings on the relation to Protestantism and capitalism. I continued with my hypocrisy speech and said things about them being sure about salvation and they say the Catholics are lost and unsure when really I had no sufficient proof that Protestants were sure of salvation either. My mom was speechless after all my ranting.

She tried saying things like God has a plan for you and you'll learn to find him some day and this and that. I nodded in agreement only to get her to shut up. We were on our way home but I couldn't stop thinking about that figure I saw crawl out the window.

‖Later in the Day

Cara's Journal

It looks like I'm going to have to leave my home. My drunken father threw such a fit today when he found out that I am a Wiccan. He is a God fearing man and apparently his God fears the Wiccan. He gave me a few good smacks in the face; it wasn't that unusual for his behavior. The man is an alcoholic after all, but it was his threats this time that really opened my eyes and told me to leave. I guess me and Danny will try to rent an apartment somewhere and try to make ends meet. I fear for my mother's life, so I placed a protection spell on her. I will have to put in more hours at Burger King and I will have to get to speed on my art and poetry.

"I invoke thee, Aradia, goddess of protection and healing. Protect her from all attacks, now and forever."

I saw Hisako after his church service; he seemed to act a bit odd. Later tonight I think I will perform a spell of wisdom for him.

Later that night

Cara was about to do as she thought she would place a wisdom spell on Hisako. She took some salt she got from the grocery store earlier in the same day. She proceeded to draw 3 circles from it. One circle surrounding the outside of the first two. The two on the inside were drawn overlapping each other. She grabbed a small knife and made a small poke into her skin releasing a drop of blood; she placed it in the center of the circle.

She began to meditate and speak the words "by my blood I call on those that have come before give him wisdom, Goddess let it be."

Suddenly something had disrupted her meditation and spell. The image was quick flash of the face of the Horned God in Wicca. It was not welcoming, in fact it was terrifying. Cara knew something was wrong; she had the feeling that the Horned God was actually fighting against her. *Had the horned God become angered with the Goddess of Wicca?* She was in fact asking for the Goddess's help. In Wicca the deities were more like symbols anyway or forces of nature but it seemed now that those forces were in conflict with each other.

"Gaia help us", Cara spoke softly.

Hisako's Journal

I have lately felt some kind of presence pursuing me. I don't know what it is but I can feel it getting closer with every passing day. Its fiery eyes burning into my brain; I feel marked or targeted by some outside force or perhaps a universal force that cannot be outrun. Things I know are going to end bad but will it be permanent is what I keep asking myself. Will it be the end? Will it just start all over again? Cara called my cell phone today and asked if I was ok and said that I was doing fine but that I felt a bit light headed most of the previous day. I didn't tell her anything about the horned creature I saw, but I have the feeling she somehow knows about it. I will see her at school today I guess to discuss things.

VI

Hisako woke up next morning and just stared out his bedroom window. He saw a few birds flying by. He could even focus on the dust drifting slowly through the air; the sun was absent from sight it was covered by the disguise of clouds passing by. Hisako inhaled a large amount of air and breathed it out softly as soft as he had inhaled. Hisako could fell the cold air of a specter behind his left shoulder and felt a gust of wind and a faint voice through the bitter air that was stinging his ears. He felt terrified for only a second and just went on about his morning like any other person. He walked a little bit to the bathroom but he found that his dad was still taking a shower; he saw him naked, but didn't shudder away from the absurd sequence, his father hadn't even noticed he saw him or even opened the door. He just closed it softly and waited outside. A few minutes later his father was out and greeted him with a "Good Morning", no reply was made to the statement; he grabbed a towel and made his way to the shower. He turned on the hot water and left his towel on the toilet lid and got into the shower. The warm water felt good upon his body and he felt as if he were dreaming again. He was dreaming the same thing he had dreamed last night. He was in a bath house with many people he didn't know; everyone was naked, but there were no stupid shenanigans like in a gym locker room before playing football. It was quiet the dripping water wasn't making a sound and they had conversations about different philosophies. You couldn't tell by hearing but just the way how their faces were formed you could tell that they were talking about just that. In his dream the words were indistinguishable but everyone understood them and was pleased to hear the frequencies of everyone's voice. Everyone stopped the chatter for a while and began to meditate like Buddhists; you could even smell the incense. He began to hear one drop of water amongst the many it came pounding down ringing in his ears. It was persistent like it consciously wanted to penetrate his concentration and it did, he couldn't ignore it. He started tearing blood and the blood dripped into his mouth; he started to choke on it and then the rest of the people got angry at him and poked him with sticks and jumped around him like a bunch of savage natives. He was no longer in a bath house, he was in a dark forest with the nude men still surrounding him they circled closer. Some began to mock him, some judged him for being naked, some just swore at him. Everything was so loud in the humid, murky forest. It was very much the contrary to the bath house and he smelled something burning and saw something burning. The fire crackled like an earthquake and the screams were like military sirens. The animals burning were a bunch of chickens with their heads cut off. The natives had their heads hanging on necklaces that they wore. He experienced this in the shower too, but in reality he was only sleeping again, reliving it. His parents heard no screams while they were watching Fox News in the morning. Hisako woke up and turned the water off and got out like normal and he was shivering. He was in there for such a long time the water must have turned from hot to cold. Hisako missed the bus to school and asked if his mom could give him a ride. She was willing to put herself to the task.

As I rode in the passenger seat, I was staring outside my window again much like the morning. There were birds flying, but their heads were loped off, but they didn't seem to notice they were just minding their own business flying. I saw a dead possum on the road and my stomach churned a little bit and then I noticed that I was already at the school. I walked out closed the door and nothing left of that.

I walked into school and all the kids were being loud, just like in the dream only without the horrible imagery. It was almost as bad though; all of the stupid people talking about their stupid movies and shows. I hate these new comedies nowadays. These comedians: Adam Sandler, Kevin James, and Seth Rogan I don't find any of them funny at all. The most intelligent shows these days were, The Daily Show with John Stewart, The Colbert Report, and even things like Family Guy, South Park, and American Dad were for higher thinking people compared to the dribble that networks showed;" reality television" like Honey BooBoo, Jersey Shore, and Breaking Amish were all popular shows and were all very dumb. Shows like Pawn Stars dominated the History Channel, but it had nothing to do with History; it's just what the masses wanted. It could be interesting sometimes but it just bugged me to see it on the History Channel. Culture was disintegrating around me in this hick town; I have a feeling that it's happening all over in America. I half joked when I begged with my parents to move because of all the redneck idiots, but inside I was, as the saying goes "serious as a heart attack." Most of the people in the school hunted on the weekends, got drunk, had sex, and went to something they called Yankee Lake; never been there, but I really never want to. I often think of the Nirvana song "All Apologies" and the line, "I wish I was like you; so easily amused." They all were entertained by the stupidest things and their brains numbed on alcohol so they couldn't think about things. Thinking makes me happy and miserable at the same time; it keeps me occupied with something, but reveals all the terrible things that the world brings.

Some hours passed and I met up with Cara to talk. She told me of how she was now homeless. She told me how her father went crazy when he found out she was Wiccan. I nodded my head to look like I was listening. I didn't care at all, well maybe a little bit, but I was a real selfish bastard. I wanted to tell her about the horned beast I saw and my dreams. I wasn't able to get to my dreams because when I mentioned the horned creature she was very fixated on that because it was very much like a disturbing image she had seen last night while practicing witchcraft or Wiccan craft whatever you're supposed to call it. I got real angry with her for some reason. Under normal circumstances I would not have been such an ass, but today I felt real crummy. All the people oh, all the terrible stupid people; I couldn't take it anymore I made a crazy outburst and punched her right in the face. I was taken away by the principle because I also started beating on other kids. The strange thing about it I was watching myself from a third perspective doing it; I wanted to stop but I was like a specter looming outside my body, like some ghost or God helpless to do anything about humanities sins. I saw that I had some kind of tremendous strength. I lifted the principal straight over my head and threw him into a locker. Some jock kids tried to tackle me and I punched them and I saw a large portion of skull fall onto the floor. I looked like some kind of maniac, but I did get pleasure from seeing the jocks all fall before me. One of the teachers was smart and called the police, but I disconnected the phone telekinetically. No one outside the building could hear the screams. I contained the sound into the immediate area. I was able to lock the doors and nothing was able to open them. I let my friends get out though. I had no hatred towards them really. I teleported them outside through some kind of wormhole or portal or something. I hardly understood what I was doing. I wasn't sure I was doing it really, but it was me; I saw him, he was right in front of me. He turns and gave me a look that completely understood everything I thought I could tell he could read my mind it was my mind but there was something else there. There was something inside me. I think it was the horned deity that I saw and felt pursuing me before. It was the cold presence I felt it was the architect of my dreams, it was my master. He held out his hand and my third perspective felt as if he were being strangled I was losing air but before it could take it all I fazed through the wall and escaped his grasp. He didn't come after me; he just stayed in there. Sitting and sitting; I could hear him snickering.

The people's minds were erased that the thing was me; it didn't even look like me anymore really. People were still aware of it and it got national coverage. The news discussed it every day. I turned my spiritual like apparition into a flesh filled human being. It took 18 minutes to complete the transformation. Cara didn't remember I had hit her so our relationship as friends was still good. We were both a bit jittery; I went to the Burger King because she had to work today and I didn't work so it worked out well. I talked to her on break and we talked about what we thought might happen. We both talked about what the news would say. We talked about how strange it was that police didn't come to the scene very quick at all.

"You would think that you could hear the sound of such a beast from quite a while away." Cara said.

"I don't know; I didn't hear a single bump after I left the building." I said.

"Yeah it's really strange." Cara replied.

"What do you think about the news, what do you think Fox's position will say or CNN or MSNBC?" I asked.

"I don't know I don't really watch that shit; I read books and the paper about current events." Cara said. "It is sad what is happening to newspapers now; they can barely even survive with the competition of the television and internet." Cara continued.

Hmm, I understand what she means but I don't know I think you're being a bit melodramatic about the whole thing.

"*I* don't know if something works why fix it." "I mean TV and the internet are just more efficient and convenient for people." I ranted.

"Well yeah but whole networks use a news station and the only people who can do that sort of thing are the very rich." Cara argued. "I guess so." I agreed. "Well, I've got to be getting home now I guess; have fun working." I joked.

"Ok I'll try." Cara replied in a friendly kind of "uh yeah right" kind of way.

I went home and at the door were my parents pretending to be all worried and nonsense. My mother was sobbing and holding me. It was so corny, like something right out of a film or something maybe like about a soldier boy coming home from the war when he was said to be missing in action or something. My dad was like are you alright son and then are you sure and then ok, but I'm open if something is bothering you. Yeah fucking right, I thought. I bet I told him I was gay his flute would sing a different tune like a horribly tuned trumpet or saxophone or something. They were like sure that I had died in the school as if they were hoping or anticipating it. They always thought I would find ways of getting into more trouble, when in reality I was quite timid about things and most certainly never looking for trouble; which I hated myself honestly for not taking risks; maybe they knew I wanted to take risks somehow and would do everything to make sure I didn't.

"If you guys don't mind I would like to see what they are saying about it on the news."

I turned the news on and saw my school police setting up a perimeter outside the building as if it would try to escape from the building. I knew it wasn't his intent; he just wanted to stay inside and wait for its prey. I saw a policeman go inside and he was thrown immediately out a window. I thought it was fucking hilarious but I didn't show it because my parents wanted me to give policemen respect and it also seemed a bit inappropriate. The whole time I was wondering what the beast was thinking and I also wondered how I was able to escape from my body. *Did I die? Was I reincarnated?* The idea of reincarnation came back to my mind as a possibility if I were. If I had this cosmic awareness of the universe could I even manipulate my soul as it was being reincarnated to stay in the same body? Plato the philosopher believed in some kind of reincarnation, and said the biggest goal was to find out what the person's life once was. I don't like Plato, but it fit the example in my head. While watching the television I was thinking, *I wonder if the police can catch him, can the army catch him; can he even be caught does he even care if he is caught?* These thoughts plagued my mind like the chirping of bugs on a bright summer day, and then all those bugs hit the wind shield when I thought *can this creature hear my thoughts?* The question kept popping into my head. I thought that it was quite a family moment in the house. My dad was in a chair drinking a beer; my mom was on the coach reading a magazine and me on the other end of the couch watching the news. We were all in the same room which was rare.

I started thinking again, can he read my thoughts as uninteresting as they are right now, but *can he read them?* The feeling bugged me like nails on a chalkboard or the pounding of a jackhammer. It was ironic for there was construction work going on outside and I could faintly hear our homeschooled neighbor's mom claw at the board. The kid next door was young and I think I could even hear him whine. It was faint to the regular person but it started sounding like screaming in my ear. A shiver went down my spine and I twitched.

"What is wrong", my mother asked.

"Nothing mom, it's nothing", I replied in zombielike daze.

And then I heard music very faint music making like ding ding do do ding ding do do. It sounded if coming from bells and there was a slightly out of tune violin imitating the same noise and I heard laughing it was a horrible laugh. It was in this low voice but it could just as easily turn high if it wanted. It sounded like a sick man sighing in his grief but this was a noise of pleasure and of joy but it couldn't make a single person joyful no; it made me want to vomit but doing that would only make it louder, it would get enjoyment out of it. I believe I knew where that laughing came from.

HISAKO'S JOURNAL

I had to take a rest from that horrible laughing that was carrying on; I couldn't stand it. I sure hope they catch whatever it is Horned Wiccan deity, Satan, myself whatever it is. I wonder how many will fall before it; I don't want to know. I can hear my parents talk about it and they are saying it's the end of the world. I don't know if I believe them or not. They think it is a sign of the end coming near, but my dad thought Obama was the anti-Christ for fuck sake. I don't know how valid it could really be. Eh, hope it gets better in the morning.

VII

Sitting here just sitting in a solitary place no one is in sight and everyone outside is looking for a fight. Should I kill them all? Would it be right? Of course not is what every decent minded person should say, but who determines what is decent? I guess I am the master of my destiny so I will make the rules I supposed, but what basis shall I do it? Should it be hedonistic based lifestyle should it make me happy all I do? Others would call me a pig, a glutton, evil and selfish. I have the power to stop their thinking, but I'd be put away; not over my dead body I'd fight and fight for my life but then they would probably kill me eventually sometime in the future.

Narrow hallway, nothing on both sides; it is bland, uncolored and there is nothing in my way nobody in my path. What if nobody but me existed? Would I somehow evolve into a being capable of creating more life so I could adapt to my predicament, but evolution takes so long create significant change? So long, way too long. Why am I muttering about it, why am I talking there is no one here to listen no one to understand just me so why not just think? Hey wait I see someone right there in front of me it is some kind of creature that looked like a humanoid. *Did it come from Mars?* No, I don't believe there is life on Mars, but maybe a more civilized and advanced planet;

one that could reach this wretched place. He comes and sees desolate waste, all gone excluding me with a blink of an eye, but he wonders why I am the only one. I said it was the war or that is what I remember. It seems most logical anyway. Perhaps global warming, maybe it was a chain reaction. The nukes start flying radiation in the air; the radiation could melt the caps. Yes, I think it could. Like Noah's flood everyone else drowned, but where was I not in an Ark, but underground escaping the radiation. I asked the humanoid where it came from. It spoke like any other human; in fact it was my own voice. He was mimicking me he was but no he didn't only copy what I said, we could have conversations together. Yes, yes, a very likeable lad, a good fellow. Then something happened; something bad, the humanoid was blasted straight in the head by a projectile. I was not the only one I suppose. I went over to greet him, but he fired. I ran away. As I ran a bullet scrapped my leg and it did hurt yes, but for some reason I had the feeling that the man expected to take me down with it. The idea of it was laughable. I hid in one of the rooms and I realized that man wasn't alone he brought others; I heard the footsteps. Clippity clop clippidy clop, yes, a series of these noises. It was louder than only one pair. They were coming into the room but I went out through the way they came in. I didn't brush aside any of them no; in fact they didn't even see me. I passed through pocket of air; I always called them air portals. Anyway, I was right behind the men with helmets oh yes, they had helmets on and armor, but that armor didn't save them, nor did the helmets. No, it didn't. I turned one of the men inside out and can you believe that all I had to do was imagine it. It was about as simple as saying a simple set of words in one's head like, the man was in the bar or the cock crows at noon. I grappled one by his shirt scruff and threw him straight into a storage compartment. I dodged the gunfire as if each projectile were only the speed of a ball being thrown at me only in their reaction time they were moving much faster than that. I chose to make it fun; I slaughtered them with my own hands. I tore them apart; it was still quite easy. I went back to my meditative state pondering on what to do with myself. I sat legs crossed just thinking and I heard another thinking. I think that they knew I heard them yes, they were scared by it. It made me want to laugh and laugh I did.

A Few Days Later

I heard a louder noise outside the building now. It was a rumbling sound. There were definitely many people out there and all coming to get me. It had me worried. RRRRRRRR, the sound kept coming and then it stopped. I saw a little machine (it looked kind of like a miniature tank) make its way on in the building and it fired more guns at me. These guns were faster but still I managed to avoid them for long enough. A few bullets nicked me but it was no big deal. A bunch of other men came from the rear entrance of the building. I turned around fought my way through them and some men from the front entrance threw these little bombs at me, these men called them grenades. They made impact and almost knocked me out cold. I kept fighting them but another one made contact eventually and I was out cold.

I woke up to a flashing light pointing straight in my face. The room was mostly dark, but I couldn't see any significant color anyway. I could perceive the reflections of light the same way that the other people were capable. Just black and white black and white. Some touches of grey perhaps, but hardly any could I perceive. I didn't particularly share that view philosophically. I had no philosophy really. I wasn't even listening to the man questioning me; he was saying something, but I was just trying to understand their whole point behind their procedures rather than on answering a question. I found the serious and important expression on his face rather humorous. I couldn't contain myself I started laughing like a maniac. He didn't like that very much and struck me with his baton; it in all honestly felt very much like a kid's plastic bat but he wanted it to hurt me; it only made me want to laugh more. He got someone to use a stunner on me and that felt kind of like a pin prick. I started to listen and pretend to be more serious. He asked where I came from and I understood his question, but it was a stupid one.

"Where do you come from?" the man yelled.

I replied back, "The same place you came from, the void; the Buddhists call it Sunyata." "All the things you see aren't real; they are just illusions brought by other forces."

The man nodded off and was saying things like "Oh brother this guy's crazy" and "we can't use this nonsense" and this and that.

I asked him "Well, what do you think is real sir?"

He was a bit baffled by the question because of it being rooted in somewhat logical analysis of what is. He just thought I was a babbling lunatic. He tried to answer it as best he could and said that the universe, the planets and the stars, the earth and all the things that he could see in person. I asked him who made those things. He said that it just happened. I then asked him how it did just happen and he goes like a big boom or God or something.

I asked, "Who made God or this big boom?"

He replied, "Well it just was there"

And I continued to ask "Who gave you these theories and all that nonsense?"

He said, "Well school and people, my church and other things." The key word for me was people though.

"So you think these "people" know the answer to everything do you? Does every one agree with them?" I continually hammered him; he nodded his head no.

"So everyone has a different view so is one right or are they all right?"

He stammered and tried to answer. He said, "Well I guess whatever fits their lifestyle."

"People have wars over these differing explanations for existence and moral teachings; do you think it's right for people to go about thinking these things?"

He was starting to get upset I could see and he was thinking *how the hell did I get into this I should be asking the damn questions?* "Ok then sir if you believe you should be asking questions feel free to ask them, my friend."

"Friend!" the man exclaimed; you killed some of my friends back there.

"What do you mean by killed?" "What is your opinion of death?"

"When the fucking heart stops beating", he replied.

"Didn't a famous scientist of this earth say matter couldn't be created or destroyed?" "Wouldn't it be reasonable to say he is still here and always here?"

"Well I am not going to talk to him as dust though now am I?" he yelled back.

"Well certainly if you don't talk to dust my good sir", I said.

"Well then there you go", he said slamming down on his notebook and exciting the room muttering "goddamn" under his breath.

A Few Days Earlier Elsewhere

Hisako is at his home getting reading for sleep. He writes an entry in his journal before resting. This is that entry.

I had to take a rest from that horrible laughing that was carrying on; I couldn't stand it. I sure hope they catch whatever it is Horned Wiccan deity, Satan, myself, whatever it is. I wonder how many will fall before it; I don't want to know. I can hear my parents talk about it and they are saying it's the end of the world. I don't know if I believe them or not. They think it is a sign of the end coming near but my dad thought Obama was the anti-Christ for fuck sake. I don't know how valid it could really be. Eh, hope it gets better in the morning.

Hisako went upstairs and took an aspirin out of the cupboard for his headache and went to bed with some difficulty. Finally he shut his eyes listening to some Adele playing on his radio. Adele wasn't his favorite artist; he liked her a bit but mainly listened to it because it was popular amongst everyone he gave into pressure with a large amount of things. He was listening to it now because it wasn't very heavy and he wanted to get to sleep. He was in deep sleep in a few moments.

Hisako was in that forest again the one he had been in before with all the savages in it only now there weren't any as of yet. He saw a group of men wandering around in suits; this seemed strange to him being in a forest and all. He walked over to ask them why they were out in the woods with nice suits. When he approached them he wished that he hadn't asked when he saw them turn his way he knew their intentions. They wanted to take him away from the forest into "civilization". Those are the words they used, but for some reason the idea of listening to them and following them brought pain to Hisako. He imagined what it was like, and he painted a horrible picture of what this dream civilization would be without even seeing it. He ran away from them, but for some reason he was moving really slow; every time he picked lifted a foot seemed very close to a minute. The men chasing him were moving pretty slow too. They were trying to run but their speed was like average walking. They caught up to me and I for some reason could move quicker once they made contact with me. I struck one right in the face and another in the testicles. The last one tried getting me, but for some reason now I seemed to have great ability, as opposed to being very slow and clumsy and all that. I jumped all the way over to a tree that must have been a few meters away and I climbed up through the treetops and jumped from each tree as if I were some kind of genetically altered super primate. I escaped the man with ease, but unfortunately he led me where he wanted me all the time out in the forest. It was very desolate, not many buildings, but the ones that were around were impressive. They were these huge industrial like buildings; the thing strange was that there were only two of them and the other buildings were made of stone and ruble. The people in those buildings got out of their tiny holes in the ground and went to the industrial sites and the industrial sites had skyscrapers attached too. They presumably went there to work and all the plants did was use nuclear energy to power things, but the people in the towns had no power at all only the people in skyscrapers did. It was sad these people were working for things that they couldn't even get themselves. I saw what they were doing with the power they were making nuclear bombs and I saw a nuclear missile come from the ground shoot of somewhere. It was confusing, because it looked as if much of the area was desolated by nuclear bombs the people faces looked burnt from some kind of radiation. Everyone looked like they were going to die. The men came out of the forest and told me to go to the factories. I saw am missile coming right back at us and there were these elevator shafts that popped out of the ground so they could go underground. People were fighting over who would use it; it was insane they were beating and biting their way to get to the shafts it was ugly to watch. The men from the forest just used some kind of teleporting device they activated from their wrist to get to what I presume is safety. I started screaming myself like the other commoners, but I did not look for safety. I just kneeled down and yelled knowing the hopelessness of survival; I looked around and noticed the forest was only 4 trees. It didn't really make sense, it seemed to be a large jungle before, but alas it was the end. I woke up before I could witness it. I contemplate whether it would be the end for real or if it would be better off that way.

I woke up to see the news again, to see what had come off this thing unleashed in the school; they hadn't caught it yet and we of course couldn't go to school. I decided on making today a day to have fun with my friends. My time was limited however for I was to work later at the convenience store. I was starting to really hate that store; it conflicted with much of my happiness; at least it got me some money. Perhaps if I got enough then I'd be happy I tried telling myself.

Hisako's Journal

I want to make the best out of today; not having school and all. The thoughts of the terrible thing in the school will plague my mind but I will try to ignore it. My mind will be focused on my friends and having fun and later be absent of thought when I go to work. Huh... Let's see how today will go.

VIII

I called all my friends: Jeff Dallas, Cara Klein and David Weiner to see if they wanted to do anything today. They all replied shortly that they did, and that they had no other plans and were all off work and all that. Jeff was always to be the designated driver because he was the only one of us that didn't drink, which was odd for the fact that I was raised Christian and Dave was raised Jewish and had it was considered immoral to drink alcohol in excess. Now I wasn't really sure if drinking in excess was against Wiccan tradition, but I wasn't concerned enough to really ask. We decided that we wanted to go to the mall and see a movie later. I reminded them that I had to work at 4 o'clock in the evening.

I waited at my house for the approach of Jeff's vehicle. I was the last one that he came for. All of my other friends were in the car. This annoyed me because I enjoyed the front seat, but what you can do I guess.

"So where to first," Jeff asked.

"I thought we agreed on going to the mall." I added.

He nodded in agreement. Jeff didn't like the mall to much really; I could see the annoyance flash across his face. He wasn't much of a consumer; it was against his philosophy.

"Eh, maybe they will have a cd I'm looking for.", he continued trying to make the best of it.

We drove for a while in the vehicle sharing an odd silence; it was a very harsh silence. It made me feel not in tune with my friends, like we had little in common. I felt insulted almost that no one wanted to talk, but I didn't want to bring anything up. I became very self-conscious in this moment that if I said something I would be ignored or shot down. So we just sat there until we arrived at our destination.

As soon as we arrived we split up, deciding to meet at the food court when we were done looking at whatever we wanted to look at. I went with Jeff, because I was also interested in looking for some new music to buy. Cara wanted to get some books; she was very into poetry but also books about fantasy like *Lord of the Rings* or *Harry Potter*. She was also fond of Manga; which are Japanese comic books. I never took much interest in them myself, but my friends along with my mutual friends seemed to enjoy them. David went with Cara. He may have been interested in getting a book but he was really a sheep that followed his friends. He didn't object too much, and when he did,(it didn't take much persuasion to get him on your side). David was also very shy and didn't like the sound of his own voice too much it seemed, when he talked it was hardly above a whisper. I personally thought this pairing was good for him; he wasn't good at even talking to the opposite sex. Cara had a boyfriend already so I wouldn't encourage Dave to make any moves, but it might make him feel more natural in future attempts.

We walked over to FYE, which was a music store. FYE stood for *For Your Entertainment*. I thought it was annoying how you had to find good music at one of these stores. Stores like Wal-Mart always had shitty music. Wal-Mart only had the really mainstream artists, and not too big a selection from their discography. I was looking for some alternative band and Jeff was doing the same. He was more into punk rock though. I enjoyed some punk, but also some indie and classic rock. Jeff bought a new Rise Against album at that time titled, B Sides and Covers. It had much of the band's rarities that didn't appear on previous albums. I didn't find anything I really wanted and told Jeff this.

He said "Fine lets go, just wait a second, I'm going to buy this".

I nodded in agreement and looked around the store a bit more and then we were out of there.

Same time but through David's perspective

Huh, what do I say, what do I say? Should I say anything? Is it necessary? Oh boy!

"Is there anything you're looking for specifically?" a voice barely audible amidst his thoughts.

"Uh no not really" replied David to Cara's question.

"You read allot of books" David said mildly reluctant. He was staring at the stack of books she held in her hands.

"Yeah, I enjoy them." She replied.

David saw she had quite a variety of books. She had some poetry by beat poets; it was like a collection from various ones. A book on witchcraft, the *Lord of the Rings: The Two Towers* and a few *Black Butler* manga books.

"Which chapters of Black Butler are you up to?" David asked.

"Oh I'm only at Kuroshitsuji 18." Cara replied.

"Oh you have quite a bit to go." he continued on with the conversation. "So what's new?" David asked hesitantly.

"Oh well things haven't been so good really my dad doesn't really want me being home", Cara replied.

"So your homeless", David questioned.

"No, not quite I go back home occasionally when my dad is at work; my mother doesn't mind so much." Cara said.

"What do you mean; why were you kicked out by your father?" David asked.

"Because he found out that I was a Wiccan." Cara answered.

"Oh……" David gave a long pause. He felt a bit uncomfortable not being familiar with Wicca and it not being particularly viewed well in his eyes and through his parents before him. "Heh, I didn't know you were a Wiccan." David said in an awkward kind of terror.

"What did you think all those symbols I drew were or the designs on my necklaces meant?," Cara continued.

"I thought it was part of an image or something you know like to be cool or something uh I don't know." He replied. They shared in a laugh after a slight silence.

"Well, don't worries about it I'm not gonna put a spell on you", Cara joked and shared in a shared chuckle. "Ok, let's find the others and see that movie." Cara continued.

"What do you want to see? "David asked.

"I don't know I feel like seeing a horror; I mean they are usually not very good, but I always enjoy them." Cara said.

"Yeah, I guess I know what you mean", David said.

The two made their way to food court enjoying each other's company on the way. David was actually learning to socialize rather well. It was a good day for their friendship. David felt more open to Wicca and realized it wasn't some evil satanic witchcraft but actually a very peaceful religion like his own should be.

A few moments later from Jeff's perspective

I was just sitting down at a table with Hisako just waiting for the others to get here. Uh, the mall made me sick with all of its flashy advertising. I am not sure why I felt this way. I just saw all the people laughing with bags full of clothes. People got their worth from their possessions and it just disgusted me. I was only making guesses of every one's intentions, but deep down I knew I was right. It is how most people in this country are. America, it is so materialistic in its culture. The people are not free they are enslaved by the markets and the things they buy, by television, by sex, by things that don't matter. I like to buy things now and again but it isn't what I revolve my life around. The only materials I get are an occasional cd or a book. I don't dress myself up to get noticed or indulge in things.

Jeff sees the others approach Hisako and himself

"Oh hey you guys."

"Oh hey Jeff; so what do you want to see?"

"I don't know, eh I don't care so much whatever you want."

"I was thinking about seeing the new Paranormal Activity.", said David.

"Really", replied Jeff "Those are getting pretty stale; the 4th one really sucked in my opinion."

"Well yeah, but maybe this one's better," added Cara.

"I don't know I don't usually like to see movies before I see the reviews." answered Jeff.

"You're too picky." said Hisako.

"I just don't care to see a shitty movie that is all; I prefer to see good cinema like 2001: A Space Odyssey or The Godfather.", Jeff said.

"I didn't really like Space Odyssey so much", replied David.

"You just didn't get it.", replied Jeff.

"Oh just shut up you guys and let's see a movie." said Hisako.

"I don't know what you want to see, Jeff?" asked Cara.

"I don't know I've been waiting to see Batman vs. Superman forever." answered Jeff.

They all agreed on that decision and went in to see their film. They were unaware of the things happening elsewhere with the creature in the school.

Meanwhile at the school

"Oh man, what hell is this thing!" rang a voice in the air. "Christ!!!" another voice rang out. These voices came from men who run into the face of danger as part of their daily job but they were up against something of which the likes they have not seem. Their minds were all racing trying to adjust to fighting this supernatural creature. *I don't know how but it feels there is something in my head speaking to me. It is saying "forget it all; forget all that you know" and then there is this slurred interference as if it were coming through a radio transmission barely making it out of a receiver. BsshBZZZGuFRSSH; then a sharp ringing pain came into my head and I screamed aaaHhhh! My comrades heard me and didn't understand what was happening and then I saw the creature we were pursuing just dash out through the door; it was so fast I don't think any of us even touch him. You're like little bugs I heard in my head and I saw him take one of my comrade's lives like it was no big deal. It was so effortless for him. He dodged our gun fire like it was nothing. I heard him saying to me; how slow they were. I did manage to hit him once, because after I heard him say that to me. It didn't hurt him much he just went like ouch or uh as if some it was just a nuisance like as it some young kid just punched him in the ribs. I thought man this is insane, I've got to get out of here. I ran away and left my men there; I felt bad about it but I didn't want to die. I was thinking of my wife and cute little daughter.*

A Few Moments later

"Sir regular policeman weaponry isn't enough; we need the military down here or something." said the policeman, his name was Jim. *I don't know why I chose to not make much caution to this coming threat, but I was getting bored of all this fighting. Something fascinated me with this particular Jim's mind. I don't know why; there was just something I liked about it. He seemed fairly innocent and didn't know much about the world. Right after school he went straight to the police force or on his way to it. He took a vocational school program. He believed in God but he never really questioned it much; the question was never asked him and he didn't ask himself. I didn't want him dead. I wanted to teach him some things. I will rest now I suppose.*

At the theater nearing the end of Hisako's movie

"AAAAAHHHH", screamed Hisako.
"What the hell are you doing", screamed some people in the theater.
Cara headed Hisako out of the theater and asked if everything was all right. "I just heard this loud yelling and all went black after that, but there was a sharp pain in my head." explained Hisako.

"You weren't asleep, and had a nightmare did you?" Cara asked.

"No, how could I fall asleep during a movie like that; it was great; you mean you didn't hear it too?" Hisako said.

"No, nobody heard anything; want to come in and see the rest." Cara asked.

"No, I think I'll just wait out here; it's almost over anyway." Hisako answered.

"Ok, I'll just stay out with you, I guess." Cara said.

"You don't have to." Hisako said.

"I want to; I've been kinda worried about you lately."

"You're acting strange." Cara said.

Hisako looked up thinking that she was coming on to him like in a romantic way, but it was only friendship. He was almost disappointed, because he got a small erection, but it shrank down pretty fast. Cara noticed slightly about what Hisako was thinking and just told him politely she had a boyfriend, and stuff, which he already knew, but it was to assure him nothing was going on between them. Hisako didn't really know what happened; he suspected that the screaming in his head was from the beast in the school. He wondered how he didn't seem to feel a connection with him anymore. *Was he dead? Did he sense his death? Could he have premonitions about such things?* It didn't seem so unusual for him to reason that for he had felt predictions before. Maybe the creature was unconscious or just about to be unconscious he thought. During the film his mind was elsewhere at some point focusing on the memories of the creature. He had no idea why he was thinking about it, but he was.

He waited for his friends to come out of the theater and drop him off at his job. He was getting somewhat anxious to work actually. For once he didn't have to think about anything. So much was on his mind right now. His sudden attraction to Cara was one of them. He didn't want his lust interfering with their strong friendship that they had already had. He was also wondering about what the disturbance in the theater meant or if it meant anything. Was it simply just a pain in his head he thought to himself? Before he knew it, he already had clocked in and was stocking the shelves. It was eerie how easily he had gotten used to the routine; he wasn't even thinking about it. He had his mind on everything else other than work, but still he was capable of proceeding to that function. It was like he could do his job as easily as any person can walk. It was an easy job but it was odd how natural it was. Especially, when in fact it was his third day on the job he clearly remembered. His work was so natural; it was not an escape from thought. He could think about things so clearly as if he was sitting down attempting to think about things.

Back at the school

"I can't believe how fast you got all this heavy artillery out here."

"Luckily for us there is a military base not entirely too far from here." "Besides a situation like this is a top priority for us."

"What do you mean" "Are you kidding officer, if we can capture this being we can do tests and if it's as powerful as you say we could use it's DNA to make super soldiers and then no one will dare be against us."

"I don't know sergeant, I am not sure that's exactly ethical."

"HAHAHAHA, oh you're serious." "Listen son, the last thing you think about in war is ethics; why do you think we are such a powerful nation anyway?" "I am kinda upset actually that were too soft to be perfectly honest, but it's all those liberal pansies that complain about it; that stops us from doing more."

Jim walked away from his discussion with the sergeant with some disgust. He also thought that this thing really wasn't something they could control. He just knew that the thing had to be stopped. He was totally against the idea of harnessing its power; there was something to supernatural about it. Jim had this feeling it was tampering with something much more than simple DNA. This thing seemed to be some immortal creature. It seemed to be that way; he saw it in the things eyes. There was some Christian voice inside the officer saying, "This is playing God" and so on. He had no power to control the operation though from here. He couldn't tell a sergeant what to do. But then why couldn't he? The rules are just made against him; what do they really mean he thought. Is it ethical to break a chain of command if the people in command are unethical? He thought of course it would be right but he just did nothing. He submitted; like a sheep before slaughtered.

Jim's Mind

My brain is pounding. It is as if there was something making it bulges out and into my skull. This creature keeps staring at me, and I keep thinking to myself I should be disgusted by the beast's appearance, but somehow I feel drawn to its presence. I actually have started to enjoy some of the chats I have had with it. It is very intelligent. I would not have expected as much, the creature took resemblance of a goat like creature. Its face looked nothing like a humans but its body and torso were pretty similar.

Its legs were also goat like. It could speak in my language, but that was not its first language; in its sleep I would often hear ranting of a language that I could make out one bit. Its roots didn't seem to be human at all. This thing I don't believe came from earth. At first I thought it was a demon, but I always imagined them much more savage. This beast though its appearance strange was very polite and civilized. I didn't trust it in full, but I began to and this made me quite afraid. I didn't know what it wanted really. He just kept talking away though about philosophies of the world and explains some of them in some detail and he seemed to favor more spiritualist type views than that of lying back on the support of a divine deity. I used to believe the contrary to his view, but I became enamored by his way of thinking. I thought about the whole world differently I began to question God and if he was real or even if this life I was living was real. My ideas began to seemingly match up with the beings ideas. He wasn't forcing ideas on me, he was simply explaining the world in a way that made sense. I could almost start reading his mind telepathically as he had been reading my mind for a time; only I hadn't even noticed until very recently.

IX

"So interesting so you believe the world is interpreted or created through mass perception."

"Well I suppose if you wish to look at it in that way; I don't like to look at many things in anyway myself." "I just simply am."

"Doesn't that bother you not knowing the answer to things?"

"No not really because what can one know outside of who they are themselves?" "Other people don't know who you are they only think they know how you should be or what you should think."

"I guess I mean society or at least our society won't really like people that do not follow the mass culture."

"That is a consequence you must not think about really it is only adhering to their way of life what can stop you if you don't even acknowledge consequence; the more you know, the more there is to remember and can't fully understand everything you have learned." "To be complete you must get rid of desire or the things that attach you to this earth; not only material possessions but ideas and norms of this world."

"I get it, but this sounds an awful lot like Buddhism."

"I would rather not give this philosophy or thinking a name." "Labels limit the potential of ideas." "Let's say you support capitalism which I highly doubt you do anymore due to our rather long chat." "You don't have to fully understand what it is to be a capitalist you don't need to be capable of writing a book on the subject and why you prefer it; you simply only have to get the basic idea and know a few things about it." "I have a view of things, but I don't try and make anything out of it." "Why do I need others to follow myself?" "It just creates conflict." "If it is given a name people can be opposed to it; it is a truth to me if the idea only originates without any chance that it can be shot down." "I am immortal anyway I have a long time to ponder things."

"Are you really immortal; can anything really be immortal do you think?"

"I only use the definition of immortality to describe it as you people know it." "I am incapable of dying as far as I know myself." "I don't know how I was made and I do not know what came first; the human race or the creation of me."

"Are you saying that you could be the projection of a human's mind?"

"Yes, I think that very likely could be the case, but I will not state that it is an absolute fact."

"Who do you think controls everything; if you were not the first being are there other things like you?" There was a short pause as the being tried to fully understand the question and put into words what his ideal answer would be.

"Yes, there are forces in the world that battle against me." "I represent something in this world." "I am the cycle of all things nature, the beasts, sex, and imperialism or the "hunt"." "Another is trying to break the cycle, another is trying to change everything and I tell you it will not work." "It will all collapse before your very eyes." "I was here first, I am the beginning, I am the way things are supposed to be." "I've seen it all except for the things before my time." "I am the God of the stars, the moons were made afterward." "Listen for I know I am right."

"What are you talking about or who are you talking about?" "The Earth goddess, the goddess of the moon; she is trying to alter the nature of things."

"How do we stop it then?"

"It is not up to me, it is up to society or what the people perceive." "I am opposed to all the people trying to change everything." "What about you what is your opinion?"

Jim was thinking about it at first, he was thinking stark contrast to what the beast was saying but he was starting to see things in a new light. The beast gave a look to the man as if he were to pounce based on the decision he might make. Luckily, for Jim he made the right decision saw it the creature's way for if not he would surely be killed. Jim's superior officer came through the door and was yelling like a madman.

"What the hell are you doing, Jim?" "How did that thing get away?" "Are you even listening to me?" he said.

Jim was listening, but he did not turn around or seem to take notice of his boss. His boss was a mustachioed man and looked a bit German; he was also a very large man. He was a thick man some may call him fat, but he also had quite a bit of muscle too. Jim never really liked the man too much, but that did not matter now. Jim seemed to be in a daze as his boss spoke to him begging him, demanding that he tell where the horned beast was. He grabbed the back of Jim's shoulder and just as quick as he pulled on him he was thrown a large distance across the room. He went right through the door.

Meanwhile Hisako is ready to finish his shift for today

"Uh", Hisako made a sigh in his head and out loud when ready to close from his job. It spoke volumes. It said he had nothing to do when he got home; it said that he would be doing the same routine some other day and that it would continue on and on. Mike Farnaby, his boss caught wind of this and asked if Hisako wanted to do something after work. He was friendly not in a creepy way but very genuine.

"What did you have in mind?" Hisako asked.

"Well, I was thinking we could go to a bar or something after work; have some nice cold ones, you know." Mike continued.

Hisako wasn't much of a drinker but he thought it sounded like fun and was a break in tradition. "Ok, sounds great!" Hisako said mildly enthusiastic.

Hisako called his family and said he would be back late. He texted it he didn't want his parents asking details and then he turned his phone off. The people all clocked out and went to their cars. Hisako just followed Mike in his car they agreed on that on their way outside. The bar was actually outside their town; it was all the way in the city. Hisako didn't anticipate this. He expected it to only be the local bar in town. The city wasn't too far away from where Hisako lived. His dad went out of town for work every day so it couldn't be too far. The bar didn't have a name; if it did Hisako didn't see the name anywhere. He entered inside and sat down with Mike and just talked like normal people. They chatted about general things and then the conversation unfortunately turned to women.

Hisako hated when things like this were brought up. He didn't have much of an opinion of what he thought about women like what his ideal person would be like.

"Come on you gotta have some kind of specific interests; I mean I know you aren't gay not that there is anything wrong about it." Mike said.

"I just really don't know." Hisako said.

"That's alright; you don't have to tell me anything about it if you don't want to." "I was also pretty shy about it around your age." said Mike in such a kind accepting tone

"Thanks for that; I hate being harassed at school." Hisako said. "I've never really had a girlfriend or been in love or whatever; I don't know if such a thing exists." Hisako continued after taking a large gulp of beer. Hisako wasn't really quite old enough to drink but Mike allowed it; he wasn't uptight about things like that. Hisako was almost 20 anyway less than two years he would be 21. Mike just thought it was ridiculous really. As long as young people were supervised, there shouldn't be a problem. Mike assured Hisako after the gulp and sense of depression that he would find someone. For the first time Hisako heard something not genuine about Mike. That statement he heard from so many people, his parents, and his friends; he knew it was just meant to make him feel better. They really figured he would down the road sometime, but they really weren't ever sincere about it. Hisako didn't believe in love; just lust. There was nothing else. Never in his life has he seen a relationship like that in a movie. Everything was just a fairy tale in the movies it was all just happy for everyone. Even in the sad films that ended upsetting seemed too positive for him. It was all so fake to him; fake bleeding plastic love. Love based on what someone did for another; love based on conditions and everyone was so nice. That is not at all what he thought in the real world. Marriages were always boring and miserable. It was either a mundane relationship or they were literally at each other's throats. He then chugged down the whole beverage and asked for another; Mike cautioned him from drinking so quickly and also his insistence for another. "Get away from me you fucking fake." Hisako raised his voice. It wasn't quite a yell, but loud enough for a few people sitting beside him to notice. He grabbed the beverage then stumbled away from his employer and chugged that beer down twice as fast. He started yelling and ranting on and some people just kicked him out onto the street. Mike tried running out after him but Hisako just kept running after being thrown out. In his mind he was just thinking "I have to get laid". He said this over and over in his head. His head wasn't on straight. Most peers would say it finally was on straight, but that was only because most people in society were either too prude or too horny. There were very few people that were in-between. He had been that way so long and was miserable from it. All the isolation from everyone, every culture and clique; it just made his head snap loose and the earlier mentioning of women just cinched it. It just put the icing on the cake some people would say. My mind wasn't really straight I was a madman wandering aimlessly amongst unfamiliar ground; I hardly visited the city and when I did it was only to do an activity of some kind like see a concert. I never really walked around in it or became immersed in it. My parents always said cities were breeding groups for impure people and said that they corrupted minds. My dad worked in part of the city; I must assume also that his mind was corrupted too. Him and his corporate banking; he sat in a desk way up in a tower staring down on the weak and downtrodden people the paraded the streets. I knew nothing of the details of my father's employment but most of the poor people didn't seem to like his type very much. My father never cared for the poor at all the idea of how they are poor always eluded him; he did not know the wealthy are the cause of the troubles of the poor. He blamed it all on the poor that they couldn't get ahead. He seemed to forget not everyone is brought up in a upper middle class house hold. I shared some of the same beliefs or rather I couldn't get his beliefs out of my head; they dominated most of my views on the matter. I knew it wasn't the truth but it discouraged me enough not to feel the least bit sorry for them and just accept they are over there and I am over here.

I was a mess; I kept attempting to run, but I lost my footing and tripped. My knees buckled and I feel on the ground. It was lucky for me that I didn't run out in the street or fall on my head. I made a very unwise decision to walk into a dark alleyway in my present drunken mad state. Consciousness was lost for a while; I felt nothing. When I awoke most of my clothes were missing and no longer had any money. Some hooligans must have jumped me or taken advantage of me falling asleep; I can't really remember how I became unconscious. I found some clothes loosely folded on a clothes line nearby; I did think for a second that I was stealing and shouldn't take them but I figured my situation called for me to take them. I didn't wish to walk around this city in my underwear.

I gazed upon a newsstand as I walked outside the alley; the sun shining brightly into my eyes. I cowered for but a moment, but then I was actually able to stare directly into its light without disturbance. My eyes turned from the sun and onto a newsstand and read the front page. It read "Beast Escaped, Officer Missing". I shivered in fear I couldn't go back home I thought my parents would keep me there and if I am rested I will be an easy target for the beast. *I know it's following me I know it's trying to kill me.* I looked behind my back every other minute of my day. I was also thinking how my parents were probably freaking out because my boss probably told my parents about what happened in the bar last night. They called me on my cell phone a few times; I reluctantly answered the phone and much to my surprise they had no idea. *I knew Mike was better than that.* I was pretty happy about that; that he didn't tell them anything. I always knew I liked the guy; he was just very down to earth and cool. I don't even think I would be fired or anything. He might talk to me about it on break, but other than that it would be forgotten. He had my number and told me later in the day actually, and said my outbursts that night would not caution my continuance of working at the store. I started to recognize the city because I regularly stopped by Cara's house to talk or whatever else we wanted to do. Cara was my only friend that lived in the city; I liked it, and though I didn't know anything about city life it just sounded exciting to me. The country was god awful boring, it took several miles to even reach any kind of business from where my family lived. Riding my bike into the small town around where we lived was quite a trek. A small trek but a trek nonetheless. I figured I'd stop by Cara's place and tell her the whole situation. I made my way to the small house to realize Cara wasn't home, but her parents were. I talked to them for a while and waited for Cara they seemed nice enough but I was getting impatient to see Cara and then it struck me I could just call her on my cell phone and meet somewhere. That is what I did.

"What is your name again, Mrs. Klein not that I should call you by that name but I am just curious?" Hisako asked.

"Mrs. Klein", a lazily demanding and playful voice rang.

"I believe he was talking to me Philip." answered Mrs. Klein. I could tell they had a unique, but familiar sense of humor with each other. I was kind of indifferent to it; I thought it was sort of funny and also sort of annoying. I could tell they were obviously bored with their marriage and kind of talked to each other in tones imitating disgust for one another when in reality it was playful and they liked each other, but no one by any stretch should call it love. Mrs. Klein proceeded to her answer in his question while in his train of thought.

"Patricia" she said.

"Oh yeah, that's right."

"But you still call her Mrs. Klein." said Philip in the same tone.

"So what brings you out here." asked Patricia.

I took a glance at both of them and decided they seemed socially liberal enough to accept an under aged drinker.

"I had a late night out drinking."

"Oh did you have a good time."

"I scarcely remember." I said with a combination of relief, humor and brutal honesty. The Klein's laughed at that bit.

"So where is Cara?"

"I'm not really sure; I don't know where she goes most of the time."

"I never see the little witch anymore." Philip added. I sighed a bit and Mrs. Klein shouted a playful expletive at him, well half playful and half angry.

"Do you have any ideas where she might be?"

"I would say maybe that artsy club down the road and to the right."

"I think I'll call her and meet her somewhere." I walked away.

"Yeah, she'll take his calls, but not her own fathers." I scarcely heard Philip say while leaving. I don't think I liked Philip very much.

"Oh Philip, stop it." Patricia answered to his comment. *Oh I should have made him some tea. What? Now I can hear people's thoughts?* I didn't feel so much like I was reading thoughts more like reading people like Mrs. Klein, I imagined she would offer me a beverage and I had the feeling the whole time she wanted to. It was like super human rationalizing based one my perception of an individual once I meet them. Sure enough, I did faintly hear her talk about it in the background as I left, but still the feeling was uncanny. *Rationalizing through the senses just like Aristotle but Aristotle didn't know about a sixth sense I don't think. I don't want to give the guy too much credit; he lived in (Ancient) Greece after all.*

HISAKO'S THOUGHT'S

I guess I will talk to my parents about being out late last night; I will keep what I was doing in secret though. I want to find Cara now though, no specific reason really, I just wanted to talk to someone that wasn't mine or somebody else's parents. I didn't dislike older people, in fact I preferred taking with them most of the time, but they just seemed too stuck in the past, I guess. Most were not conservatives per say, but they were stuck on a democratic neoliberalism and capitalism sort of view, I realized no one believed in it deep down, but were made to think they did. I liked to think of myself kind of a progressive but I really didn't do anything to support my claim. I was just all talk, mostly. I don't really like the idea of capitalism and patriotism towards the state like we were to respect where we lived more than anywhere else. It's just a matter of where we were born. I don't think anyone knowing some of the history should be proud of America. The slaughter of Indians and slavery and the caste system that followed and the great struggles to get it through, and we claim our self to be a country for rights to all and tolerance and shit, but we don't have a very good history of it from the start since Columbus came in 1492. I laugh at the notion of patriotism now; I used to embrace it I guess from what I am told; I have no recollection of it really though. I don't really know how many alternate realities there are. I am not sure if they are real or I am just seeing the way things could be through a dream. Maybe my thoughts represent a dream right now. Well here is the place they told me that Cara might be.

X

I looked around the room and saw a lot of hipster type yuppies. They were talking about lot things that I was thinking about and it went in the same circle, and it didn't reach outside the sphere of thought. I just looked around and it all seemed so fake to me. I agreed with it all, but it was all too obvious. I don't think they wanted to do anything about America, but just wanted to talk and bitch about it like I have done. I could imagine myself sitting down with them, but thought they might mock me, I didn't know the technical jargon surrounding the atrocities in the country and what it did abroad. They just seemed snooty to me or pretentious, snobby despite the lack of income. It baffled me and I thought that it was counterproductive; it was just pushing some people away from what they wanted, this attitude. I looked around some more and saw Cara on a stage with a band speaking in words I didn't quite understand. It was very strange music her band was playing. The guitars sounded funny like they weren't tuned the right way and some of the "lyrics" weren't even words it was just a bunch of sounds. And there was this other person in the corner messing with electronics and making loops of speeches made by people varying from Martin Luther King Jr. to Adolf Hitler and the voices were looped backwards and forwards during breaks in the music. I didn't really get it, but it released emotional feelings that I couldn't explain the root of, there was this deep intensity building inside of me like getting choked up and about to cry only no tears feel, I was choked by the awe and epic scale of controversial undertones mixed with artistic spontaneity and anarchism. I didn't expect it because the music was so strange but I learned to like it. Cara's singing voice reminded me of Patti Smith's. I know Smith had some odd music as well, but I listened mostly to what was popular like Because the Night or People Have the Power.

As the group had wrapped up their songs; Cara was offering the chance to purchase a painting of hers. I didn't know my friend was into all this artsy stuff, but I thought it was pretty neat. I knew she was very creative, but I didn't know she made it into a second profession. I motioned to her and let her know I was in the audience after someone purchased the painting. It was kinda odd to me the painting that is. It didn't look like much to me but I didn't get a very good look at it. Cara saw me and we had a seat at a table. Her boyfriend was the guitarist of the group and sat down at the same table. She asked me if I enjoyed it and said that I did. I was a bit too accepting in my response for I didn't completely love it or even like it from the start. I just wanted to be nicer than usual. I started to have an excruciating headache that I couldn't stand and I had to request a trip to the restroom to clear my head.

My head was throbbing like crazy; I fell to the ground and started losing consciousness. I seemed to be falling or the air seemed to be rising I wasn't truly quite sure which was happening and then all was blank. Before I knew it I was now inside a small grocery store. I was just walking through the place alone. The fluorescent lighting was beaming down on me and the cursed buzzing of those lights annoyed. I remember going into this store, but it never was quite the way that I remembered it now. Their pharmacy area was much larger now. In fact it seemed to be most of the store. My parents were with me, but not from the beginning; they surprised me with some video game nearing the end of our trip to the store. Then we drove away from the store we hardly shopped for anything really. We got in the van and just drove and I was in the back seat just looking back at the store some reason we seemed to move away from it very slowly; in fact it almost seemed as if the store was trying to catch up towards us as we left also. I couldn't prove it but I had some gut feeling. I was starting to get a headache again and then I feel unconscious. When I woke my parents were still driving me but we weren't driving back from the store because I didn't see my video game in the van. My mother was like, "Oh good you're awake, do you feel alright" and so on. I was just thinking *that trip to the grocery store must have been a dream but it seemed so real.* I was trying to remember when I passed out previous to the dream and remember being at that beat nick club, in the rest room. The day previous was the first time I have had alcohol really and it was hard for me to get used to its effects (it didn't help that I got totally wasted my first time. My parents luckily didn't know about that. If they did they would be saying "you know you must have looked like a fool" and stuff. They were real concerned about how they looked to everyone else and seemed to want to preserve some kind of a name our family had and I was thinking *We are just people no more special than anyone else no less.* I definitely thought people took themselves too seriously.

Everyone thinks they are so important and insulted way to easily like if insulted it's, like how could you be like that to "ME"? It made me sick it was very pompous and self-absorbed. Even though my parents frowned on sex before marriage they would have been glad if I had a woman by my side when drunk. They were ashamed that I didn't have a girlfriend and were worried they wouldn't get their grandchildren and whatnot. My father in fact would always point to random girls on the street and it was rather embarrassing because he was trying to make me care and the relationship wouldn't be the same. I didn't get the concept of just going out there and trying to love anyone. I just couldn't morally try that route; I had to genuinely love them or like them from the start. I still was holding on to stupid religious teaching like someone's out there for everyone; God has an Eve for every Adam and that shit. It was very romantic in my mind, but the time never came; it was just a way to keep children from having sex. To cling to blind hope that one day they would find love whatever that is. *Love, what the hell it is anyway.*

"I'm fine mom." I replied to statement of hers that I didn't really hear.

"Ok, no reason to get so angry." "Where were you last night?"

"Oh, just at Cara's house and no we weren't having sex, dad, besides she already has a boyfriend."

"Why should that matter you should show her that your better than that other guy." He had this stupid macho man aspect to getting girls like he wanted me to go out of my way to try to impress them in some way and I didn't want to look stupid. In a way I took myself too seriously in that way but I just said I was too humble.

"Well what did you do anyway, Hisako?"

"We went to this club, I don't know, where she like played in a band."

"I didn't know she played in a band."

"Yeah, her boyfriend is the guitarist and she is the singer, I don't know, it was pretty interesting."

"Why don't you do anything like that?"" I mean you like music and everything.", Hisako's mom exclaimed.

"Well yeah, but I don't think I'd be good at it, I don't know." added Hisako.

"Well you better try something, you can't work as a stock boy all your life; no son of mine will be doing that forever." warned Hisako's father.

Well, technically I am not your son. "Whatever.", said Hisako in a hardly audible voice.

"Whatever!?!; stop the van!!!", demanded the father. The vehicle came to a sudden stop. "Don't you ever talk to your father in that disrespectful tone of voice!"

You're so full of shit. "I'm not really even your son; I'm just adopted because you didn't have the testes to make one yourself."

"You son of a bitch!" yelled the dad.

"You hear what your husband called you, mom?", Hisako replied jokingly.

"You shut up you fucking smart aleck!"

"No, no just stop!" My mom started crying; she didn't know what to say or who to side with. My guess is that she hated how both of us were acting. I shared the same opinion, but I was just so angry.

"You get back here!" my dad screamed as I exited the vehicle. My mother continued crying; while my dad got out of the van and made this big scene and then just got back inside once he realized how foolish he looked and I am supposing told my mom to just drive back home. I had a feeling my father disowned me at that moment.

Later the following day
Local Newspaper

An article appeared in the paper. The title said in bold **Man Commits Suicide after Rapes Wife**; it was straight and to the point. At first glance, seeing the headline is of little surprise. People die every day most people think. It certainly is normal for most people anyway. The picture doesn't show the faces of any victims involved only the police investigating an incident near a house. There is yellow caution tape, police cars and the actual police officers in the picture. The address and name of the people involved is mentioned in the article. There is very limited mention about how the rape occurred but enough has been obtained from the victim to identify that they were in fact raped.

A 36 year old woman was raped yesterday by her husband aged 48 in a home in Ashtabula, Ohio. According to the police they received a call from a woman that sounded scared from the woman's cell phone; the police said "From what we heard she was breathing heavily and said that her husband attacked her." Details on what caused the fight were not released to the authorities. The police didn't get to hear from the husband because he committed suicide afterwards when his wife told him as he found her hiding that the police were coming for him. She said, "He was stammering and couldn't say a thing at that point he was pacing the room and asked me if I wanted to die with him." The woman requested that we didn't release her or her husband's name to the public. The victim police said suffered from a broken rib and minor bruises.

There was very limited information in the paper the articles were never very large on information. They didn't say much about anything; the paper was a breaking industry; everyone got their news from television which usually had a bias on every political issue, reported murder, or pointless drivel that wasn't important to hear.

Hisako read the particular paper and realized the two people involved were his parents. He had no reason to suspect, but only a feeling and knowledge of the area in which they lived. He felt a cold chill; he wasn't afraid but cold to the situation in general; he didn't really seem to care but for a few seconds. He didn't speak to anyone that evening. He didn't even think much; most of that evening he just sat on a bench and stared into the distance.

An astronaut's view from space

I see something; it's this bright light shining out from the earth. I wonder what it could be. It seems to be coming from the earth itself but I have never seen a light like that anywhere. He kept contemplating what the light from the earth could be. He thought at first it was the return of Jesus Christ for he was raised Christian as are most Americans. He had a feeling it was something else entirely however. He couldn't explain why he disowned this theory; he just didn't understand because he was a Christian and all Christians were to be in Heaven before "Christ's second coming." Did being in outer space stop the rapturing to Heaven process; he thought.

Was it a mistake to go this far outside the place God put us. Did society go too far from its home God made for man and woman? He dreaded the thought of being left behind especially in space. He was thinking all this within a span of about 30 seconds. He thought that the light could have been aliens underneath the earth waiting for the moment to come to surface. He was going off of various stories he heard to explain the light. He wasn't using rational thought nor could he because it was something unlike anything he had seen before. He felt a lump in his throat. He didn't want to live through thinking all of this; it was too much for him so he escaped his space suit and lived no more.

Hisako felt this kind of serenity as he stared into the sky he could see the sun starting to set and forgot all of his problems about his father committing suicide and in fact it made him glad deep down. The world looked so bright through the sun set. It was at least bright for him anyway. There was something radiating from his body; it was a substance nobody on Earth knew except perhaps Hisako, he was the one experiencing this light. He was thinking about how the whole situation happened with his mother getting raped and his father killing himself. It all flashed into his head like a dream.

"I can't believe our son; he is so ungrateful the sunova bitch." He could hear and see his dad saying it. Mother was still sobbing like some stupid bitch that watched some cheesy movie and started crying with Kleenex's and everything.

"Stop it, stop." She would mutter under her breath most likely because she just didn't want to hear anyone say anything about their little boy like that.

Yes, it is all coming to me father would stop at a red light look over at her and start badgering her, the bastard and calling her a "dumb broad". They would later stop at home whilst arguing still and them mother would say something that would go to "too far" as if they were wrong in saying something against his opinions or liking. He would then strike her once maybe twice enough to land her on the ground and then he would rip he clothes off clumsily the fat out of shape bastard and take his pants off as well of course and the raping would commence. He whipped out his penis, such a small little thing I'd imagine it. He had ambition but he was spineless. He was just another businessman he was like everyone else so it was easy to get where he was. If you want to handle money, people in America will help every step of the way but heaven forbid you be a poet or a writer or musician. You have to get rid of all you have and go it alone and get a break. I thought it was dumb how people used penis length as a measure of masculinity. It isn't a very logical thing besides what is wrong with being sensitive or a bit feminine? I never understood it really; I have said this to myself about a million times, but I despise macho men. I suffer because of it. Enough about me, my poor mother got raped. Well she would probably scream and grab for something to hit him but not before he would plant a seed inside the "dumb broad". Down crashes the vase upon the bastard's head. "You bitch!" he would yell and my mother would run out the door and my father chase after her and trip on something and she would get away. He would meander around the house being depressed a few hours perhaps maybe watch a television program and get frustrated about how entertaining it wasn't. He would turn it off wander around in the basement maybe find a rope and contemplate killing himself but what way would he do it? I really wonder? Hanging, no too complicated I don't know if he can tie a knot for it, but maybe. It would take too much time though. Tying the knot, finding a chair and something to hang from, by the time he did that he would forget all about it. Poison perhaps, razor or knife maybe, but I think he would use a gun. Its quick painless for but a second and it's not close and personal. Yes, a gun would probably be his way out. He would point it towards his head and" bam!" he would fall right on the floor. I am almost certain it would go exactly like that. Aahhh! UGGHHHHH!

   I just threw up on the floor; blood I think. Now I just feel kinda crummy. The light isn't here anymore. It has left my sight. Was it ever really there? Was I dreaming? It did seem really wonderful. I just don't know anymore. I am worried for what I feel has happened; it is hard to explain, it is though I absorbed the impact of a nuclear missile somehow contained it unharmed and released it into the world. That is the best way I can explain. I don't want to think anymore. Most of these thoughts; I am putting in my little black book my journal. What a great shock it would be for someone to read it, I think.

HISAKO'S JOURNAL

Again I am writing in my little black book. I don't really understand the purpose of it. I guess it sorts out my thoughts, but what will I be thinking to achieve. What is at the end of this thing called life? Have I seen it already? I had a dream last night; it was mostly blackness, but I saw an orange ring. I can see this when conscious even if I close my eyes but it was so clear in my dreams. I understood everything it meant whatever it did mean somehow, but all I can remember right now is that it was an orange ring of fading light. I tried my hardest to focus on it to get to the end of it but when I got through I would see another ring and would focus on that one. I don't know if my body was in this dream. I felt a consciousness at least there was no mirrors but that shouldn't have been a problem for I could just bring my hand in front to see it. I didn't seem to have control over any part of my body but I did not feel restrained. I felt freer than I ever had; I have had this dream many times. Many times there is nothing that feels spiritual about it, but every now and again my mood changes. I wonder if anyone else has had this dream; it has occurred constantly for me. I often get frustrated that I can't tell people about a real interesting dream; dreams are things I often like discussing and when there is not much to be said, what can you say? Then again what can you say about anything that hasn't been repeated hundreds of times to the point of exhaustion.

XI

I was wandering the streets approaching the city again which is a place I have rarely been. My parents wanted me growing up outside the city and didn't want me corrupted by outside influence. I would almost say it is more corrupting to keep me in this rural area with the television and internet as the only thing connecting me to the rest of the world aside from going to school and taking me out on occasional errands or a nice dinner. I always felt so alienated from others I can't tell what is more dominant; the psychology or sociology of myself. Is it something about my genetic makeup or is it more the society my parents put me under. It is both of course but in this instance I would like to again try and find out what reason applies more.

There has always been something about the city that attracted me to it; I think more than anything it was a sort of rebelling against my parents' type of thing. They preferred the country; the people there were more conservative. I have grown to not like conservatism and I strain away from liberalism too. I am not any kind of ism; the world to me now seems meaningless. Many people might think the things I have seen give me more reason to pursue things. I have no idea what the things I saw were. I could just be having delusions that feel incredibly real. Politics is a weird thing; you can make it the most important thing in the world or the butt of every joke. I have done a bit of both but now to me it's just there. If all the people are provided for what have they waiting in death another life to go through the same things or be denied paradise for rejecting an omnipotent being or be buried in the ground. I have my theories on the afterlife and believe it could be a mix of things. I have the feeling I have been reincarnated a number of times. I have died in my dreams before a number of times and when I wake up I feel different then when was the day before when these dreams occur. I feel alone with this sort of feeling. I can't read minds but I can almost sense no one is on the same plain of thought as me. If many people came to these realizations wouldn't you hear constant talk about it? Conservatism just seems wrong; it's just a way to justify the rich getting more and the poor getting poorer. The Republicans and Democrats are hardly different; to me it seems that the democrats want to have rich people stay rich and poor people stay poor but Republicans seem to ironically be progressive in both areas rather keep things at a constant, making the rich super rich and the poor super poor. I guess I might call myself a socialist and say spread the wealth so no one is miserably poor, but the rich people would try to find a way to manipulate socialist systems wherever they emerge. They would hurt the social programs intentionally and ruin their people by paying a group to aggress against them and blame it on a faulty economic system. The same I believe happened to the Sandanistas in Nicaragua, but I do not want to discuss politics to you reading right now or maybe I do. Like I said before I don't see the point in any of this conflicting against the powerful and I don't want to live with it really either all I can do is do the best I think I can to promote what I think is right. If in the end it does nothing to benefit people, no harm no fouls. At least I tried making a moment better for someone in a moment of their life. I really have no right to talk like this though, I haven't contributed to any of these types of political movements or forces of which I speak. My friend Jeff does all that stuff. He is very politically active at least in a limited way; he pays what he can to grassroots organizations and bitches about it to people on the internet all the time. Maybe I am afraid to fight for these causes, but I don't see a reason to fear fighting. I like to have fun I guess, but my life isn't fun so why not do something? I guess when I get down to it I just don't care enough.

I started feeling a bit faint, so I sat upon a bench and dozed off a bit. I nodded out a few times and had that vision of the orange ring in my dreams. Flying, flying, flying through the ring I told myself. I wondered if people could hear me saying this in my speed sleeping or if I was just saying it in my head. I was feeling some kind of ecstasy or passion or desire, but it was a limited feeling because once I got through one, I immediately wanted to get through the next. The capitalism was engrained into my thinking even in my dreams. It's the constant pursuit of more and more; the American dream. Anyway, I awoke what seemed like a few seconds later, but in reality was most likely several minutes.

When I awoke I found it very odd that I was able to sleep so sound for there was all this commotion and yammering about. Everyone looked so busy going where they needed to go. A mad fat woman came up to me and asked me if I knew Willie Nelson died. She had gray hair but wasn't old, she was one of those people. She said she wanted to tell everyone so they wouldn't be sad; for one thing I didn't know Willie Nelson was dead. I agreed with her and said that I knew he died and that I dreaded for her passing to make her feel not so alone. I guess that's really what she was trying to do for others who were fans. I particularly don't think I am a fan of Willie Nelson, but I never really listened to him so I usually say he is "ok" when the people want my opinions. It was all very strange, there was a sick looking bearded man on the road and he was asking for money and he was pushing around a shopping cart; for a tick, I imagined that the woman and this man had been married at one point or the other and pretty much lost their homes. The man at least, was clearly homeless and I couldn't be too sure about the woman but my imagination wandered. I couldn't get my mind off of this concept for a while and then I realized that it wasn't so busy where I was, there were less people than I imagined and then it wasn't the city I was in. In fact it was only the side of a freeway. I watched the wind blow across the trees. I couldn't hear it and I couldn't feel it, it was a very faint wind. I almost thought at a time, I was only imagining the trees move because I stopped believing that the wind was really there. I pretended I moved the trees with my mind. I started to realize the people I had seen were not there anymore. I didn't feel like there were much places I could go, the land was large and open, but I was afraid to move anywhere, like as if I walked passed some boundary of places I would blow out like a candle. My sensory features were shot I really couldn't feel a thing and I started realizing that this was probably a dream and I wondered how I couldn't see it before. I blew out like a candle and was back on the bench.

It surprised me that I was already in the city; it was close to where my parents dropped me off. I saw a woman that looked similar to the one in my dream and she was with a man and they seemed perfectly sane. They seemed like a nice couple and had a few little ones with them. They weren't the cutest things I ever saw, but I liked watching the little ones tug at shirt of their mother and demand that they be taken to some store. It annoyed me afterwards, but at the time it seemed funny. Little kids asking to do more and more things, the greedy little buggers, I thought. Children are really very greedy things, only they are greedy in ways that only hurt the wallets of their parents and not the lungs of someone passing an industrial site, or when the world eventually floods over, but I digress. I had to just get off of that bench and to some kind of destination, but I was already unimpressed with all the flashy lights and signs the city had. It was getting dark again and thought about how much of my day I wasted but then had a second thought, about how in the world could I make it matter at all. It started to rain a bit and I really told to myself that I needed to find some place to go. I hated rain when it dropped onto my skin or hair; I want it to only hit my clothes. It seemed to rain more and more in the past few years. I made grunting noises as I looked for a place to eat, I was very hungry. My clothes weren't for rain and that added to the discomfort, I had to stop telling myself all this because it only clouded my focus. I saw an nice enough looking place to eat, it wasn't fast food, but it wasn't quite so very fancy indeed. It was just a city diner.

I walked inside and heard the bell on the door ring behind me and that annoyed me a little bit for some reason, but I shrugged it off because it was nice and warm in contrast to the outside, no rain or anything just fantastic really. I sat down and my waitress gave me a menu, I requested some breakfast food, but they said they didn't serve it at this time of day. That bummed me out a little because I really felt like some eggs, toast, hash browns and a nice cup of coffee. I then looked again and said that I wanted the pasta and requested to have it without meat in it. I was starting to fancy the idea of becoming a vegetarian, it sounded just right. The waitress said "Ok, anything else" and I said that I wanted a glass of water. She gave me a looked and I was confused what it really implied, *was she annoyed with my request? Was my order taking long? Did she not like the idea of vegetarianism?* I had no idea really. I waited for my food looking at the so so artwork on the walls. It was done by people in the area and it was not that should be in a museum, but it was well just art like any ordinary picture or something. It was all landscapes. That kind of art annoys me; I like it when art is a little less clear. I like it to have a story, to mean something. Most of these, I can just see someone sitting looking at something and then painting it, no story, it was just good, bad art, if that makes sense. Their skill as an artist was pretty good but the expressive aspect was absent. I really liked stuff that made you say "what the fuck is that!" Salvador Dali painting always caught my eye; they were beautiful and just plain strange. Nothing in the painting was something the man saw if he saw it he was either on drugs or dreaming. Yeah, but all these paintings were so plain. I looked at everyone eating and this was a common practice for me I don't know why I did it; I guess I like to observe people. I saw a father argue with his son about religion but not in the way I expected; the father was saying that religion was a joke and the son was saying it was for real. The newer generation is supposed to not believe in rubbish, not the other way around. In a way, I felt sad for the kid because he was told he was wrong. It was like someone telling a very young child of five or four that Santa Claus didn't exist. It ruined the magic of his imagination and hopes. It let me down, and I didn't know what to think or say.

"Yeah there are a lot of very nice stories" I heard the father say implying that all they were just stories and nothing else. He brought one up and the son knew exactly which one when the father was a bit foggy on the details. It may have been Jonah in the whale or Zacchaeus in a tree, I had no idea which story it was I forgot. Then my food came and all of my thoughts about the two melted away like the Persistence of Memory. I tried putting back the pieces, turning back all those clocks of distant memories stretching farther and farther away. The time could not be manipulated; the clocks melted in my hands and fell into my lap. I imagined I actually, had gotten eggs instead spilled the plate onto my hands but not I had the pasta on the table before me. Before I knew it, the father and son left the dinner, *who are the father and son what do they look like I forget.* The persistence of my memory has collapsed and now I figure that it is about time to dig into some pasta. That pasta tasted wonderful, it was like I could hear a symphony in my head as I chomped away at it. I like classical music but can't really identify the pieces so well. I realized that the pasta had meat in it and it really let me down. I am betting that the symphony was Beethoven's 9th and couldn't eat another bite. It had to be the 9th that is the one Alex Delarge in Clockwork Orange heard when he saw Nazis bombing. I left without paying and ran as fast as I could nobody noticed and no one saw.

I continued to run and didn't see anyone new and nobody seemed to notice I was running, but I guess that just how things are around here. It didn't seem anyone cared, the least about my wellbeing not that I was asking for it, but if I was hit by a car or something I don't think anyone would care. I think I would; I hope I would anyhow. It would have to happen for me to be sure. I was still running whilst thinking all of this and I started to forget why I was running or I had no idea where I was running and where I was headed. If the sun were ahead, I would have went straight in. I stopped and recollected what I had of my wits whatever that really means. When I stopped, I felt that was cues to have everyone stare at me, but no one looked but I felt as if they were. In fact, I held my hands up in the air as if someone were going to arrest me in fear of my feeling of paranoid thoughts of the stares. I passed a beggar asking for some money; I wasn't sure what he had in mind as a proper amount but I gave him about five bucks and he wanted more. He even started clawing at me, the freak, I thought to myself, "Get away!" I screamed. People looked for a bit as if wondering why I was freaking out and not giving the poor man more money, but I did give him money and it was almost all I had. It made me feel bad; I didn't feel greedy like they wanted but it was if they wanted me out of their city, I felt unwelcome. I started running again to find somewhere safe, away from all the people.

Cara's Journal

I've been thinking about Hisako and I am still worried about him; he seems different to me now. He seems to be drifting outside our world as if his mind were levitating beyond his body some of the time. I also feel that there is something now watching me after the day that there was a problem at the school. It doesn't seem threatening, but inviting in a way like it wants to tell me something, but contact is hard to make. I have been thinking about attempting to make contact; mostly I have been trying to ignore it but it is starting to become more present and also more difficult to simply shrug off. I have talked to Daniel about some of this and he is just as confused as me and suggested what I have been thinking to do and that is contact whatever this thing is. Hisako and whatever this is seems to be attached but I just don't know how. scribbles.......

Cara's mind

What the? What the fuck? What are those things? Where am I? Everything is all hazy. Uh, shit, damn why am I so clumsy? That horned beast is coming after me!!! Oh, shit! Phew good thing that thing is here to help. Hey, wait I have a feeling I know these things. Aren't these those things, the ones that I believed in, I don't know. Wait what. Huh. I'm dreaming I think. Uh what no? It feels so real. Mostly in the dreams I can't feel things. But I felt falling down but I can't seem to speak. I don't usually hear myself in dreams but yet still I can feel objects and feel pain; that's very odd. Huh what it's coming at me but not the other one now the one that helped me out but what oh no huh? Uh, I guess it all was just a dream. Nothing seems different. My posters are all in place. My books seem fine as well; all my records and cd are in order. Yes, everything seems to be in order. I don't think my mind is in order; no yes it is, yes it is everything is just fine doing worry your little head child. It is all going to be fine. Somehow I'm having trouble believing myself but it almost feels as if I am not arguing with myself. I'm just asking for an answer just please help me now.

I hear nothing, no response at all. I guess I'm on my own. Yes, that's right.

Hisako's mind

I keep thinking about my mom. Should I feel guilty for making my dad in such a rotten mood, no I don't think so. He is a rotten bastard. I should visit my mom it's only a matter of time. A matter of time before she kills herself as well; she can't care for a child alone assuming my father successfully landed a seed in her. It's funny in a way; if that were true it would have been his only child. I am not even his true son. I am only related by name but no genetic match or anything. I am going to go back and comfort her I think. That would be the "correct" thing to do. Yes, I will go do that.

Story pans over to Hisako's mother

"Where did I go wrong Lord", she cried out. "Please guide me in my time of need" she continued. She started to cry questioning the existence of her God. Reality had hit her; she did not have a husband to stand beside. She wasn't a very independent woman, her traditional ways made sure of that. She didn't want to go back to the church. She was thinking of what they might say. They would judge her and say it wasn't a rape. She was being promiscuous. That was pretty accurate of what they would say. She was also thinking a great deal about having an abortion, something she had been very against the idea of when she had her husband's security or God to lean on. She felt just alone now. It was her and only her or rather her against the world. It all happened so very fast and then there was a ring on the telephone." A message from heaven perhaps?" She might have thought, but no it was something more comforting and much more credible. It was her son; he brought her comforting words and said he would be right over. It would be difficult to explain how much weight had been lifted from her at that moment. Everything now seemed as if it would be alright. That is what it seemed.

Hisako's mind

I need other people. Maybe that will be my goal for the rest of my life just to help people. I don't see what this world can give me really so I'll give to others, yes, that should make me feel much better. I feel so limited though. What can I really do by myself? I can't rely on others; I don't know many people too well or not well enough to collaborate with them. Perhaps Cara or Jeff, maybe; I don't really know, I'll think about that later. I've just got to get back home. Man that feels corny. I have to go back to mother, she'll be my shelter. Why should I care so much about appearance? I don't know anyone, who cares what strangers think? I feel like I'm committing crimes if I do something on my own. I can't feel I can be independent without it being construed as some kind of sin. Why does this sheltered lifestyle control me so? I can see things others can't I perceive dreams more clear than others. I am conscience it is a different reality, when I am asleep here I wake up another place and the same happens to everyone else, they don't know it. I feel so damn alone.

XII

"Out of my way kid" someone yelled as Hisako bumped into them.

This annoyed the shit out of him. He wasn't much a kid anymore he thought. He was about twenty years old. He could admit young and inexperienced, but most certainly not a kid. He was additionally insulted because he just felt smarter than most people and felt the label "kid" implied that he was stupid. He wasn't stupid though he was bright, but not so much street bright. He bumped into a woman whilst distracted from being irritated with the man he previously bumped into on accident. It would be almost humorous to watch if it happened on television. He said sorry to the woman he wanted to be polite and was told to be extra polite to women because they were lesser beings in their parents' eyes and needed more care. That's how his parents were taught and that's how he was taught. An inherited sexism passed down and while it faded each generation a little bit still existed. Someday it would vanish perhaps. Hisako would like to see that day but still unknowingly feel into the trap of tradition from time to time. Then while all this went on in his head he tripped on the sidewalk, but this time not interrupted by another human body just the pavement. He felt very clumsy, as if in one of his dreams. He sometimes had dreams where he was very physically incapable, others quite the contrary.

He got up and shook it off. Thinking to himself get a hold of yourself just walk, don't run watch where you're going man. He felt a cold staring eyes looking at him and turned his gaze to the other side of the street and saw a policeman. He didn't trust policemen, mostly because his dad always bitched about the tickets he would get. He didn't hate them; he just didn't like them too much. He had a feeling the cop was looking at him. He didn't commit any crimes he thought to himself, why would he be after me? Am I just being paranoid? But no the cop started chasing him and he started running again. Luckily, he didn't feel clumsy anymore but still he couldn't run very fast. He felt like he was going very slowly, even though he tried with all his might to get away. This cop was catching up to him fast; was he just fast or himself really slow. He judged him distance by the locations he was passing up. He figured that no one was moving too fast and that he was moving incredibly slow. The cop seemed to move slowly as well, but not quite as slow but still it seemed that it took too long for him to reach Hisako. Eventually the police officer caught up to him, but Hisako was able to escape his grip. They were tripping over each other; it was quite embarrassing to watch but it seemed very heart throbbing in their own minds. Time seemed to move in slow motion between the two of them. It was either that or everyone else was moving slowly. The crowd interpreted everything going on at normal speed though. As the cop finally got a firm grip on the young man he vanished into thin air.

Hisako didn't simply vanish and disappear, but reappeared in another place away from harm. He didn't want to stay there for long. He had a feeling there was something different about this cop as though he thought something unnatural. He felt him inside his head much the same way the beast pestering him before had. He realized he was right outside his mother's house actually. This was convenient because of course as mentioned before he had been meaning to get there. Hisako walked through the door and into the living room where his crying mother sat.

"Are you alright", asked Hisako.

It seemed just really odd to ask a thing such as that, her husband committed and being a traditional wife had blamed it all on herself. Every problem was hers and if her husband did something wrong, she had something to do with it. She heard her father say to her mother similar things. She adopted the ideas of her father and those ideas were passed down through her mother's submissive old fashioned 50s housewife style, (the nuclear family look). Hisako hated it because his friend Cara was a feminist and he liked the idea of equality between genders but didn't really think about that too much. He thought again and then asked with more sincerity and looked into her eyes. That was hard to do because she kept turning away and he was not to comfortable looking at people when he was expected or thought he was expected; it wasn't hard if he didn't think about it but that never happened. He never gazed into anyone's eyes on instinct. Hisako put his hand upon his mothers and raised it up and held it firm cherishing the touch of another human. They started to weep together and then hugged.

"Oh, Hisako," his mother bellowed out.

Meanwhile in an unknown location
in the mind of the beast

"I don't know what to do; he evaded my scent, my mind, my control?" "What happened?" "I thought my powers were near unlimited, he is only a simple child with mental problems." "Just go use common sense his mother's husband killed himself and his mother is probably taking it hard; this boy has a kind heart, of course he went to see her." "But, no I can't go there, it's too close." "Too close to the moon, it will shine there soon and we hate the light of it." "Yes, we hate the sun, but the moon much worse." "Love shows itself at night; no don't call it love, its lust, it is a terrible thing, we hate to see it. The passion the enslaved us; it turned us into this beast." "There is nothing to worry, this child has no passions, and no one has passion when they think they can't do anything about their circumstances." "I suppose there is no harm, but the Moon goddess will see us." "We must plan somehow in a way that puts us at an advantage." "We could use a disguise and get to Hisako and try and change his thinking that benefits to get him with us." "We can take a form that he trusts perhaps one of his friends, but no he knew that you are in my body." "We can distract him by sending a visitor under our control." "No, he would sense that too." "Come on he is just a fucking human." "We've got to make him leave the house for that is where his friend will be and that is where the threat is." "We can use his workplace, can make one of the other workers sick and their boss will have to call him in, yes, that should work."

Back at Hisako's mother's house

Ring! Ring! Ring! "I'll get it" Hisako told his mother

. They left a pretty good conversation at a fairly good time and everyone was starting to feel comfortable, the tears had dried upon their face and everything was going to be all right, it seemed.

"Hello, Hisako, it looks like you are going to have to take Gerald's shift at work. He came down with something that seemed pretty serious."

"Does it have to be today?"

"Afraid so, and sorry if you don't come in we are going to have to let you go."

"Yes, ok I understand, I'll be right there."

He knew that his boss wasn't sorry for asking, he seemed like a nice guy but that would probably just stay at work. His boss didn't care two shits about what he was going through. He told his mother that he had to leave and go to work and she understood; it really wasn't such an inconvenience for her, she was feeling better now and felt that they could be a family again and function as such and just go on living. She watched him as he left through the front door. She was happy but started crying anyway. She ran out to him and hugged him again and the hugged real tight and passionately like as if they were lovers or if Hisako was leaving to fight in some war or if he thoughts of family had been extinguished entirely and he would be gone forever.

"I love you" she said in a tired but soft voice.

"I love you too" was the reply, as he passively left the social interaction they shared. She went back into the house and looked at the picture of their family when they had all been together as a unit and she turned it face down, sat in her armchair and grabbed for a tissue box because she might need them as her thoughts wandered.

Hisako noticed as he walked the ground looked like it was moving not as if an earthquake was occurring but it was all much unsolidified. It looked like it was breathing as an elephants chest would. It was moving up and down slowly just like the previously mentioned personification. He was wondering what this could mean. *Am I hallucinating from lack of thirst? I haven't been drinking much water lately. But is it something else? Is someone playing with my head or am I controlling this?* He saw stairs forming from out of the ground and he walked up them until he was above anyone's view. He could somehow breathe perfectly well despite how high he was and he saw a figure come from the clouds. It was the bastard cop from before but he could react faster now for his situation was odd as this occurrence right now and encouraged him to act quicker. Strangeness allows one to be ready for strange thing he thought. He ducked out of the way and almost slipped off of the steps he had climbed. Though Hisako was quick the creature was quicker and grabbed him by the throat and asked for his surrender.

"Why are you after me?" yelled Hisako.

"You already know that." answered the beast.

He was right.

"I have the answer to the world's questions.", Hisako told him in an unconfident manner.

"That's right, but I am here to protect you.", said the beast.

"Oh, then get your hands off my neck." demanded Hisako.

"Sure" "You are some kind of higher human." "Your scientists would call it evolution but it is more than that you seem to have a unnatural way of adapting to the environment and you are also adapting the whole world to itself. Things seem to look terrible but they aren't. Where you live everything happens at the center the tragedy is just in your mind and it is tearing your community to pieces. The people around you are sharing to your view of the planet, the news, the television; you don't even have to watch it you just adapt to it because people are saying it." "You can sense the pains of the earth and you try the best to get them going right." "Everyone has a different view of the planet, everyone has different experiences, but I am not sure you understand to what extent this goes." "You have died at least three times in your lifetime and you wake up at perhaps a different age or different place every time it happens." "You may have expected some of this but when you fall asleep you have only been transported somewhere else while you remain still in your bed. All these worlds are interconnected and the different dreams you have are interconnected." "You can sometimes be awake in two or more dreams at once and while that happens, what you humans call luck is working well for you in those moments." "Part of you somewhere in another world falls asleep when you make mistakes based on that world's rules; it is I guess like karma."

The creature gave Hisako some time to think about what he was just told. Hisako started speaking. "So what does it matter if I am correcting my world; if everyone else's world is different."

"But you know everyone else's world and therefore can manipulate it, but you are suffering in every reality you are placed in because the other forces want you out; they don't want to move ahead."

"What is this other force?"

"It is the moon goddess."

"Cara told me about that; it's some Wiccan deity, but I thought she was good and gave regeneration and rebirth of souls for the living; who can argue with that?"

"Regeneration and birth of souls, that is what you have got; it does not apply to most of the rest." "It is also keeping you from unlimited power; your ability of rebirth saps ultimately your unlimited power."

"If my power has unlimited potential then couldn't I over power her now or stop her from sapping my power?"

"You must get the goddess impregnated." "She is called the eternal virgin; if you take that title from her she will lose her power."

"Well then who is it; where do I find this moon goddess?"

"You can do it by having sex with any woman; the spirit of her is within all women."

"Where is your place in this, what are you?"

"I am the horned deity your Wiccan friend told you about." "I am in the entire world."

"Then do you just want to do this to get yourself power?"

"Yes, but look at the threat that is present." "Are you tired of living and not succeeding, because of what she has made this world, she gave you a gift but it is more a curse than a gift isn't it? "You wake up every day wondering if you died somewhere else again and seeing the whole world at once not actually seeing it, but feeling it and all the things that could happen, but you are there to clean it all up." "You deserve a break you have done too much for this world; you should experience its pleasures and take the reins."

There was a short pause, and Hisako thought about it and he was tired of feeling second class and finally decided yes he did want power. He wanted the things promised to him and they were rightfully all his. That is what he believed, yes, it had to be true.

"Yes, I agree, let's do it."

So he grabbed the beast's hand and shook it; he no longer wore his disguise and Hisako could almost instantly feel a strain on his body, not enlightenment. He just forgot about it and fell down towards the earth, but slow enough where it hadn't injured him. He realized he had a message on his phone saying that he was fired from work basically. Hisako didn't know what to make of that. He was happy for the most part. He went to a corner store and picked out a bottle of water. He was thirsty. When he opened the door with the water, he heard something that sounded like a thunderstorm. He was that thirsty perhaps, that his head was just pounding and every sound happened to upset his ears due to a lack of water within his mouth. His mouth was dry and his breath smelled like crap not literally it was only an expression. He was thinking

Do I fulfill the promise?

He was thinking that it was weird that out of all the religions the Wiccans were right. All this seemed to happen after he questioned his Wiccan friend about her beliefs did these encourage him to form a world where Wiccanism was the true oasis and answer to the questions. *Can I stop this whole thing after it has started? Is there any way out of this?* Asking questions didn't seem to help for he loved it too much and to do anything about it would rob him the excitement of asking these questions. Would they become his demise?

Hisako's Mind

My mind is racing and nothing is really chasing it. I feel as though nothing can catch me now. But still I am told that I am in pursuit; so I suppose I must hurry. I have to find a mate to plant my seed so that the virgin Goddess will be impregnated and I may live forever but what is the point of it? It feels as though I can live forever anyway; it has even been revealed that I have already died a number of times. I am hanging on the words of someone. I had no intention to trust before; I ran from his path constantly, but it leads me to a dead end and now he had caught up with me, but to protect me from what I have learned. The Goddess is evil then; I must realize, he didn't kill me, why would he take all this trouble to warm me if he meant me harm to not kill me at the moment he had his hands around my neck. Is there another motive that he is counting on and is I his puppet? What can I do?

XIII

I could sacrifice my body to the Goddess in the case that the sun God is not telling the truth. It is too risky. I could be what this world needs. I could be their God, but do I want to be a God? It sounds dreadful, but how could it be you have no responsibilities. Too much power takes away all responsibility. Nothing can make the whole world go to ones wish not even for a god. I can think uhh are these things gods? Are they figments of my imagination? I have decided I will go and I know who will be my target. Hisako went down off his platform to the ground. *Now where would she be?* Hisako had a specific girl in mind that he wanted to have sex with. He never liked her and that was the point; he always felt self-conscious about having sex with someone he loved. He didn't think it was right somehow, even when that girl may have been anxious to have his seed. He thought she was attractive for sure but she was too stupid for him, they had nothing in common and he knew a way around the decision. He thought to impregnate someone who was surely not a virgin. This girl was definitely without a doubt someone who had had sex before. It was Brittany Wilson, a girl from school he knew. She was labeled a slut even among the sluts. Hisako even noticed that she had seemed attracted to him but this he could only tell after someone had pointed out to him. Hisako always wanted to think of girls not as sluts. It fell in line with Cara's and Jeff's feminist views. There was the adage that women or girls were always considered in American society prude or sluts and that there could be nothing in-between and they all wanted to prove that wrong, no matter how much in vain it seemed. In this circumstance however, Hisako saw her as precisely what she pretty much was a slut.

A sharp pain met the ear drums of Hisako. He knelt down to recover his wits. He noticed he had a message from his mom on his phone telling him to come home because work had called the home phone. It gave the residence the news that he had been fired and also she had news of her own to give him. He was thinking if he should travel home. It wasn't a long walk but could any distraction be acceptable? He decided to just call her on his phone and get the news from her that way.

"What is it?" he spoke in an annoyed tone.

"Oh, honey I just wanted to tell you that your friend, Cara, stopped by to check on you."

"Oh ok thanks, uh I am kinda busy."

"I thought you didn't work?"

"I don't, I am just doing some favors for some guy in town, you know because I don't have a job I figure I've got to get some cash somehow."

"Oh such a responsible boy, I love you."

"Love you too mom."

Well that's the end of that. So where do I find Miss Wilson?

Hisako went down the local town where all the middle class people were. They were lower middle class, but it wasn't a ghetto area. He saw a newspaper rustle on the ground. He wondered if anyone had read it or read more than the sports section anyway. That is all anyone seemed interested in he thought. Kids might eye on the comics, some might be interested in their horoscope, some might be interested in an unusual story that happened recently in the area but most people were just interested in the sports sections. This bothered Hisako a lot, particularly because he really had not the slightest clue about anything related to sports and he felt isolated in school because of it. He wasn't sure if this was the blame, but it was a theory. Well anyway, his mind returned to what he thought he wanted to do; he saw the faces of the people passing by, some wouldn't turn towards them, some felt afraid to look, some looked angry and disturbed because Hisako would stare at people when he thought he knew them somewhere. He didn't know most of the people, but it became a habit of his. The people weren't depressed, but they just seemed to exist. They didn't want anyone in their business and no one really asked to be in their business. It wasn't about fear, but a conditioned belief amongst people in this area or in America. Everyone didn't seem to trust one another, there was an air around them that said

"We must do this on our own." It was the spirit of American capitalism Hisako thought.

No, they didn't look depressed, but not really happy either; they looked oblivious to anything other than what they have been doing.

"Can I have that real quick?" Hisako looked up and saw a man. He was middle aged and not particularly attractive; he was not skinny, but not well built or fat. He was like most people a average looking person. He wanted the newspaper under Hisako's shoes.

"Oh, of course here you go."

The man sensed obliviousness in Hisako's voice like he was distracted with thoughts not even thinking of the man but heading to another spot as quickly as he could after he got through talking to this guy in front of him asking for the daily news from underneath his foot.

"Is something the matter?" the man asked very kind.

"Uh, I don't know, have you just felt like the whole world just might collapse on you any second like I don't know?"

"Uh yeah, I know what you mean."

The man had some confusion with the way in which Hisako put his statement, but he just simply took it as life rough for him at that moment in the young man's life. They both took a comfortable seat on a bench outside the strip and began to talk about life. He started talking about how he used to be married and had a divorce and how that really hurt him inside; his kids were taken away and everything, but he kept himself busy and sane by keeping himself occupied with hobbies he created for himself. He became fond of blogging and wrote articles in the local paper and got a dog, took it for walks on occasion and sometimes had breakfast with a few old friends. He made a habit of coming to the same diner every Sunday morning. He talked about times he would chat with them until it was time for the place to close. His point was really to just try things. Do what feels just right, not in a hedonistic indulging yourself with pleasures way, just making a simple, comfortable life for yourself. Not so much giving up on dreams but simply living. It sounded all well and good to Hisako, but his situation was different. He thought it was different, or was it? He continued to think back, and ask himself, *can I make my own decisions?* Hisako didn't do much talking mostly listening so the man left him when Hisako ran out of things to say.

He did say after man left, "Hey, thanks for the chat."

"You're welcome." came a friendly reply.

All of this made Hisako think a bit more. *Should he continue to heed his visions call? What is the worst that can really happen to him? He could be killed. The earth may be doomed? What purpose do those things serve in the final analysis?* That view was somehow comforting to Hisako. He thought at one point or another the world could end would be punished would anybody suffer really? Would any really suffer in the end? Would the stars learn to speak and make conspire to make something new? Is there really a God? Are these apparitions Hisako see really them? They are the Gods of the universe of the entire universe? When they were gone did they talk to some place else? Do they govern another region as well? He came back to the thought they were only illusions that he had created. Why after he knew an inch of Wiccan faith did he perceive these celestial beings? Would he ever find out without any prior insight? He chose to give up his plans given by the "Sun God". He was going to have his own life.

He looked up from the bench in which he was sitting and started and saw the rays of the sun reflect off of the buildings in the town. It was a very beautiful moment for him and now it seemed like he absolutely had the answers to everything. Then as he noticed it getting darker a sudden feeling of doubt came over him, but then he forgot everything got up from his bench and press on no not pressed on he was strutting as, if he had gained some kind of great victory. Like a hero coming back from the war if they acted glad after the war in real life but that was quite doubtful perhaps more like a soldier in a war movie. Across the street were a few police officers. They were looking in Hisako's direction and they pointed out at him. They walked towards him and asked him to show them his ID. He didn't understand what this was all about but he showed them anyway.

"We suspect that you may be responsible for the murder of your father; we believe that the suicide was faked."

"What the hell are you talking about?" was Hisako's reply.

"We noticed the suicide note was not in his hand writing and we're just trying to ask everyone he knows; your handwriting matched the note the best.", they accused.

"This is ridiculous I wouldn't kill my father."

"Sure you wouldn't." said the lower ranking officer.

"No honestly."

"Then you should have nothing to worry about in court then." the same cop replied.

"No, No, stop!" Hisako yelled. Some people looked at the situation and turned away; it was none of their business, besides he was probably a criminal they all thought. It was generally accepted that nowadays young people were responsible for several tragedies and only they themselves were, no other factors play a role, young people are just becoming insane and there is no help for them. This is what the news seemed to be telling people nowadays, with all the reports of school shootings and whatnot. The police officer struck him with his baton and then all was blank.

Hisako woke up in the police officer's car in park doors locked. The cops were on break and decided to have a quick bite a fast food joint. These cops didn't do thing by the book really; they had a history of unprofessional police work, but it didn't affect them. They didn't get in trouble for any of that. They regularly targeted black people, but they also made deals with the dangerous ones involving drugs, guns, and prostitution so that they could just turn a blind eye to the crimes they commit. They were planning to bring Hisako into questioning in the station, but while in the restaurant they planned to both be the bad cops and brutally interrogate him somewhere where they couldn't be seen. That's precisely what they did. Hisako couldn't say anything about it because he legitimately knew nothing but they just didn't buy it. They lacked any proof also, but the letter which was mysteriously written in Hisako's signature.

"Ok we're getting nowhere with this", the higher ranked cop said.

"So heh, let's just talk real civilized like now."

Hisako spit not on an officer just getting blood out of his mouth.

"So you really have no idea about your father."

"Yeah, he just killed himself he was just real upset; we had an argument and he kicked me out and well he raped my mother and I guess he felt really guilty because of all that and didn't know what to do; I wasn't really living with them at the time. I was just kinda trying to be a nomad and not stay one place long just wander the earth you know."

"Yeah, yeah so what was your relationship with your father?"

"Well to tell the truth I really hated him, but I didn't kill him; we disagreed on everything though, he was nothing like me; but I didn't kill him."

"What about the note then."

"I honestly have no clue."

"Huh well I don't know what to tell ya kid."

A few hours later Hisako was brought to a cell to be held for the time being. It was so strange; he did know how all this could happen. It seemed like five or six hours ago he was the happiest person alive, but now he would probably be a jail bird. They couldn't really prove him guilty, but he couldn't afford a good defendant and they probably had a good prosecutor. What the hell could he do? He was guessing to tap into his mind and shift things again or wishing for the help of some other being like the Sun God or Moon Goddess. It didn't matter. It seemed all his life he tried to do nothing or simply hope for the best and those just simply were not constructive. He had to do something now. He had to get out of his cell. He kept repeating it to himself gotta get out, gotta get out, but nothing happened.

Hisako lost the trial that was to come and is now in prison. It wasn't even close everyone feared young people in today's society, they were blamed for everything. Hisako didn't like prison, but who ever does really. He didn't see any way out he would just have to wait for the sentence to pass. The other prisoners treated him horribly; they chose him as a target because he was weak and young. He was actually raped one night. At night he cried himself to sleep and in the morning would see slop that he was expected to eat. He chose to abstain from eating on a few occasions, but eventually got so hungry that he had to give in. Hisako was on good behavior most of the time despite being a target. He tried sucking up to prison guards and everything. Five days past and he found out that his mother had also committed suicide presumably the assumption she had no life beyond caring for a son and her son would be in jail for a long time. Hisako decided that he wanted to escape even with nothing to live for on the outside. The prison wouldn't allow much; all the books in their library were uninteresting and he was getting psychologically murdered in the place but how would he escape? He just decided he would make a run for it when no one was paying attention. Eyes were everywhere though. He needed a distraction and who would serve his purposes; he was a victim after all.

The next day they wanted to made the inmates do exercises. We really didn't want to, but the guards insisted. I spat on the guy's face and he struck me in return and pulled me away. He kept striking me and the other guards tried pulling the man off, but I found the strength to do it on my own somehow and then I struck him in a precise spot that instantaneously incapacitated him. I don't know how I struck the right spot, but it felt I had all the time in the world to do it and I somehow had the knowledge of what would work best. The other guards crowded around me. There was one sneaky bastard that stuck me with a pin prick and I fell unconscious.

I woke up again, but not in a different spot this felt real I was forever stuck here I thought. The walls surrounding me were all white; they thought I was crazy, but I wasn't I just knew too much. It was either that or they were clueless about so much. They asked questions again, but this time I didn't answer any of them. They were frustrated by my lack of volunteering; they thought I was a cocky smart ass which I suppose was quite accurate. I felt pretty stupid at the moment however and that was getting on my nerves so much that it seemed my fury was being projected outside the white walls of my padded prsion for I heard yelling and screaming on the other side and no more questions were being asked through the speaker phone they had in the ceiling. This was probably due to the fact that these people were too busy screaming. The walls around me came falling down and I walked through the flames that tore them down. I went at a steady pace no hurry really I felt nothing could no stop me. what contrast between now and a few moments before. I found the sneaky bastard that pricked me and I gave him some of his own medicine right through his eyeball and then I ripped his balls off; I found it especially suitable somehow for him personally. Several guards and even some of the prisoners advanced against me because they feared my power, but they all were lifted off of the ground and vaporized into thin air and before I knew it everything around me was sinking except for me and I simply walked out of the prison as the walls that surrounded fell into the earth like quick sand. I was free but people were on my tail. It didn't matter much because they fell like the walls, straight into the ground. I didn't feel sorry for any of them; I proceeded to go near the sky; I was like Icarus now but would my wings soon melt? They hypothetically did not however. I was for real free.

I didn't see the sky, only the clouds and they were dark clouds, like before a storm but it wasn't going to storm because those clouds started to open up. The sky wasn't bright, though it was just white, not blue like you see in the movies or cartoons just plain ordinary bleak sky and it would turn black as the sun sank behind the horizon and the stars would show themselves on the countryside. People might look up and question what may be beyond those stars. Some people think it is blacker some think it is white beyond the blackness and golden too. I think it is blacker but also think that there are other worlds. Some of them are perhaps our dreams or some are other planets with strange kinds of life. There might be all the things we imagine in fictional literature and fantasy tales. What will happen when all the ideas are completely controlled by the minority of the population are these fairy tales keeping it safe or will they collapse on us all followed by bombs or commanded by them. It's all speculation but what could the truth tell of our future?

I began to descend to the Earth and it was a beautiful view as the tiny buildings came closer to my view. I didn't realize the great altitude I was at prior to descending, I didn't feel the wind blowing on me and it didn't seem harder to breathe either. The horned man rose up with me, but I gripped him by the throat and threw straight into the earth. Something got inside my head and felt like knives; it was the Moon Goddess trying to get inside my head. I thought back mentally and I swear that the impact tore her head right off. Allah came for me, but I ripped his flesh into pieces and Buddha floated above me and he took me somewhere else; everything was white and there were leaves rustling around me throwing me about throwing me into invisible walls but then I brought the Buddha to the sun and I survived somehow but he burned up. The Christian God came to thank me and greet me with a handshake and a smile; I took his hand pulled him close and stabbed him with a rusty blade. Nothing could stop me. All the religious deities of the world fell under my control, now I wasn't sure if these were simply some kind of self-defense mechanism I mentally constructed for myself, or if these things were literally there. I was as powerful as I ever could be; I had no one to answer to not even nothingness could stop me. I could explore all the possible universes that may have been out there, but I went back to my hometown to live a happy life; the happiest I could possibly have was my mission. The success must be mine. The world's standard of success in addition to my own. This would be a simple task now I thought. Existential egoism should be a simple task to fulfill being the only God around. No "Gods" intruding on my activities; what is a God; I can't even acknowledge what it is. I would create a utopia all for me and I think it would be best for the rest of us; if I could only get their support in this. I have to get them on my side. What happens when they disobey? I'll think about it some other time.

As soon as all this realization was coming to Hisako, as soon as he realized, no Gods, people, or states could stop him much of the world's chaos had spontaneously increased. He was the absolute authority there existed such a thing now if there hadn't previously been such a force. All the people of the world were now expected to be slaves and to be honest it was probably in their best interest. .... Perhaps.

A Palestinian husband holding his wife
tight hiding from missile strikes.
An African American is stopped by a cop on the
road; the cop busts his tail light and puts drugs in
the seat, pulls the man out and beats him senseless.
An anti-islam British nationalist group beats on
Muslim civilians in the streets of London.
A drunken husband beats his wife after she
tells the children to go to bed because she
doesn't want them to see their father drunk.
A homosexual is made fun of in school inside
the restroom. He is forced by classmates
to kiss a girl; the students all mock him in
the presense of his embarrassment.

Detainees in Guantanamo are tortured and
beaten though some are completely innocent.
On a New York City Street a girl is raped in an alley.
Westboro Baptist church protestors are in
front of a government building in efforts
to halt legalized same sex marriage
A man shots himself because he can't pay
his taxes and fears prosecution.
Environmental activists attack people from corporations.
Police beat peaceful Greenpeace protestors.
Someone overdoses on heroin.
Someone crashes under the influence.
Someone crashes while texting their gang
members to take a hit on somebody.
A girl's father yells at his daughter for getting
pregnant; he gives her the belt on an Alabama farm.
A man sexually harasses an employee in a corporation.
Workers in china die of exhaustion while
working slave labor wage while knitting a
sweater for Walmart Corporation.
A man hangs himself in prison. ... Hisako smiles

Hisako's Thoughts

God is dead; as Friedrich Nietzsche said but God is not dead. To say he was dead would imply that he had been alive at some point. I will live my life as if I were a fictional god as it were. I am enlightened now. I am meant to have everything; I was born with this right to power. I must pursue my interests and no one has the right to stand in my way for I know what is right for everyone but I don't care for them. If they complain that is their problem. I know the minerals that make up money and could project it perfectly from thin air as a counterfeit but I will play by the world's rules not because I have to, but to humor the attempts of others all the more. I know the stock market and can predict what will sell and what won't. I can get rich by simply sitting and calculating everything perfectly. Selfishness is not immoral it is my will against others and mine is incalculable. I was born with it; I must have been meant to have it for a reason but no there are no reasons I just came to learn these things on my own. I am self-made. If there is to be a "God" I am it.

XIV

I pass by the statue of Atlas in New York and something inside me rises like a phoenix. I feel liberated from ideas and morals. There are no limits. Ah, America the land of opportunity, if your rich enough to buy it. I am rich enough now; it has been awhile but I have milked money from the stock market and now I can obtain all the pleasure I need all the things I want. I don't find pleasure so much in the things but the exciting potential that I can obtain through infinite knowledge.

In the heights of my mansion I am sleeping with several women at once. Their bodies caressing mine with such skill; they have certainly done this before I imagine and I can adapt to all their sex moves perfectly. The orgasms almost bothered me. They were so loud; I don't want to hear all that. I don't want to hear all that but I let them have their fun, I mean they were making me happy anyway. After we were done we all had some fine tobacco. *Ahh, exquisite cigars from Cuba.*

I went to the most elegant eateries in the United States. I gorged myself on oysters and fine steaks and the rarest wines. Oh, I've always loved the color of red wine, so passionate, so lustful it reminds me of blood. I am not obsessed with violence or death or anything like that, there is something in the comparison I find romantic somehow. The tastes of this dining so savory and sweet, the sensations of a job well done it seemed but I didn't feel as if I did much of anything, this seemed all too easy for me obtaining all these riches.

I seemed to get a gathering within the stockholding circles at Wall Street and they thought my champion of capitalism could lead to economic growth in the country. Yes, economic growth for the capitalists not the workers, but I played along with it; I was after my interests not others. Why my life must be put in debt for someone else; if there is no God there is no reason to be generous to others. "With great power comes great responsibility", I remember hearing that phrase from the Spiderman comics of my youth but it means nothing now. My great power should be for my interests and it would only be responsible to look out for me because giving to another only keeps them down because the ingrates won't learn for themselves. They need to motivate themselves and not wait on God's to give them blessings. The people need to will themselves to power being nice won't get you anywhere as far as wealth is concerned. The highest moral good for me is to look out for my interests.

I became famous within short time. I was a young star in the realm of wealth and some power. I started my own company and I made my own religion it was all a lie but it was a way to suck wealth from the mindless hundreds and later even thousands to have believed it. The Christian extremists called me the anti-Christ and I supposed I can't disagree I am as I before admitted against what Christ stood for. Jesus wasn't really a selfish guy from what I remember from those stories but these lunatics are fucking hypocrites; most Christians are about as greedy and capitalistic as I am. I created many advances in technology that would make Steve Jobs and Bill Gates jealous and I used my company to profit off of it. I used laborers from across the seas just as the other companies did for me. They were job creator's yes but many of those created jobs were not from American workers and were from poorer countries so they were able to pay them shit wages so they could make more money for themselves but the rest of the American economy suffered while the rich keep their money. Exploitation for the good of themselves, yes that is capitalism that is the true American dream.

Several years past and a lot of rich voices were asking me to run for president. I ran as a Democrat to get the people's vote as well as the votes of business but my policies were extremely conservative. I said I was a Christian and supported marriage equality but wasn't over enthusiastic about it, I promised that people would be treated equal in the workplace and pretty much said everything that people wanted to hear. I got some of my own people to stage a terrorist strike for which they made that which people call the ultimate sacrifice and I blamed it on someone else. The people ate in the palm of my hands and with my advanced technology the military weapons because more sophisticated and we didn't just get the people supposedly responsible I used it as an excuse to take the civilization over and I made a statement saying, "These people can't be trusted to handle their own government, they are savages, who have no respect for human life, we must govern their country and protect the civilians from further terror." It was a ludicrous statement but some people were all for it. There were dissenting voices but I had them quieted and their names erased from history.

The people served the rulers for years and years, but then eventually they got feed up and all the businesses suffered because the workers had suffered. The factories all shut down and I didn't do a thing about it He was wrestling with something of his own. When it all started you couldn't go anywhere without a riot and then the masters of the sweat shops and the manufacturers of war feel to the people's wishes. There was no wealth and no poverty money soon became useless and all the people planned to overthrow the cause of all the suffering even though no there had been none without Hisako's mind conscious of anything that was happening. The business men didn't act without with his command in the past years because they just became accustomed to worrying about threats that had happened or thought to have happened there were tales of it anyway. A small group of rioters headed to Washington thinking that he would plan an onslaught of the workers.

Meanwhile Hisako ponders his actions and is aware of the attack to come, he writes in a journal contemplating everything that has happened to him, all the things he had done, all the lives he put in jeopardy on his behalf. He had met his past self or perhaps his future self or himself from another dimension or universe. He warned him of the attack though he already was aware of it but he was more simply telling him as a judge or a call of his conscious for the seemingly had none at this point. He heard all the yells of the people suffering and he heard how the people started laughing again as they brought down the government ruled by corporate interests. His conscious personality told him to write an epitaph of some kind to mark the time of his death or to serve as some sort lesson or reminder of what happened if there was anything to remember because it felt as if the world was falling down upon itself. The people seemed to be enlightened as Hisako had become disillusioned by his power and how it's attempts to please him were discovered to be in vain and he didn't understand what more he could do or what could make him happy and then he thought maybe that wasn't the answer may be the answer was to serve but how could he serve when a God was alive, for a God must be served. What would the people do when he fell from existence would they know what to do when they were all happy without any kind of class. Would they feel as though they could go no further or would they be content with happy bliss, is a life without conflict worth living? Why serve? Why oppress? Oppression causes more sadness than serving does if serving causes sadness. Perfect unity what a foreign concept, was it possible, it could not last under answering to a tyrant. He went through this cycle of thinking whilst writing his "epitaph". They were at his door pounding and pounding in fear he made some of the people evaporate into thin air and he feel on the floor and pounded his head on the ground as if he felt the horror that the others on the outside of the wall did when they saw their comrade bite the dusty trail. He started choking on his own blood and died and he took the world with it.

HISAKO'S JOURNAL

In a moment there was a ringing in my ears and enlightenment in my head. The songs from the Heavens or whatever they are called were absorbed by an impressionable mind and then all the answers in the universe were mine. Endless desire couldn't nourish my hunger nor knowledge or power. The best thing to do would have been ironically sacrifice it all and do nothing at all but observe what will be because everything is preordained; to sit like a Buddha with inches of space to live and endless contemplations, dimensions, and places to witness without even the move of an square inch or whichever measurement you would prefer whilst reading this entry if anyone is alive to even see it. It was all in my grasp but the more one travels, the more one tries, the more one learns the more everything seems confused and lost. Everything is doomed always was, always will be and no one is to blame. It is neither a God, nor the people living their lives. As I write the whole world has turned against me; its people are coming in waves of hundreds, but as they get closer they vanish in my midst. I am not controlling this it is just the way it had to happen. Whole countries and continents will be swallowed in my presence. Once everything is gone I wonder if I should continue a new world so these catastrophes can happen again. Only time will tell whatever that is.

XV

Now there was nothing, not any kind of organism in existence nor was there any kind of material thing nothing that took up any mass of any kind. But then there was a little light in the far distance of what most would call the void. It was an orange light blinking. It persisted to do this and then it stopped for a moment and a beam projected from it and it sprayed out some kind of white mist or powder into the air and it became dispersed throughout corners of this empty space and made barriers some areas had pockets of oxygen and some didn't and other some orange mist projected from the orange blinking light and chemicals were other elements were dispersed some known by Earth's inhabitants and some from other galaxies that were never yet discovered by Earth and out of these elements formed chemicals and some blended in the right way to create stars, moons and planets. The planets and stars were not in full form yet the more complex planets took longer to exist and the ones that were mostly gas were old. Some planets were inhabited by vegetation and some from this kind of organic metal capable of growing much like a tree, shrubbery or plant. Some planets were made of water; sometimes the water was capable of thought. Some planets had air that can think. Some had thinking plants. On the planets some bacteria formed and virus's and sometimes the bacteria and viruses were the size of a full sized rabbit on earth and sometimes they were even bigger. The same scenario happened to insects in different universes. Fish formed on some of these planets and beasts and humanoids of all kinds. Some humanoids looked like the aliens people on Earth usually called fictitious and others looked like things beyond human comprehension. Some planets worked like the theory of evolution and kept producing new forms of life as the planet changed the beasts changed and adapted to their worlds and on others life could not live or adapt to changing conditions some planets hardly changed and the beasts all stayed the same. The humanoid creatures usually started to question and to think of the outer limits and what was beyond the confines of where they lived, and some used reason to concluded what the answers may be but some made up myths about Gods that controlled what happened and some believed their planet was the center of the universe almost seeming afraid to acknowledge there could be something out there more advanced than they were. Some organisms were given the gift to experience knowledge of things from different worlds; mostly they experienced these in their dreams. These cycles kept happening and even the unreasoning people learned to reason pretty well and developed ways of understanding the world around them. Sometimes they came to wrong conclusions, but those conclusions were based not of Gods but of themselves of reason. Some worlds created great weapons that ultimately ended their civilization and sometimes dissenting voices interrupted the use of these and they survived a bit longer. Perhaps one of the planets inhabitants will join together to trek for life on other worlds and find some and continue a never ending quest to discover the universe in its entirety. Maybe one day, maybe one day. The world continues, though nothing is real.

END